AN ENGLISCHER'S FOLLY

THE AMISH QUILTING CIRCLE

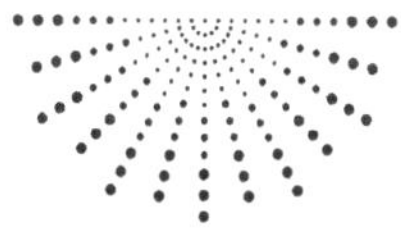

SARAH MILLER

IRENE GLICK

SWEETBOOKHUB.COM

CHAPTER ONE

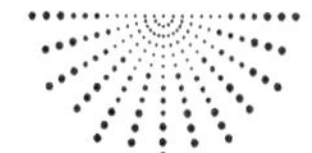

Naomi Troyer was humming to herself. It was a beautiful day in Faith's Creek, and she was walking to the market with a large basket under her arm. She paused to watch a bird singing in a tree above and smiled as it flew ahead of her as though leading her along.

"Are you coming to the market, too?" she asked, as the bird now perched on a fence post by the edge of the road.

The bird chirped and flew off. Naomi smiled and counted her blessings, thanking *Gott* for everything that was hers. She was blessed with a loving family, and a happy home, and she had just begun stepping out with a delightful young man. His name was David Glick, and that morning, Naomi intended to surprise him at his market stall with a batch of apple fritters she had made fresh that day. She had got up at the crack of dawn to bake, and the scent of the still warm fritters wafted up from the basket.

"He's going to love these," she told herself, as she came in sight of the marketplace which lay at the center of the community, and where several dozen stalls had been erected, already with customers bartering and bargaining.

"Good morning, Naomi, it's a beautiful day, isn't it?" one of the stallholders – Joseph Sholtt, a friend of her *daed's*, called out.

"It certainly is. Have you seen David?" she asked, and the man nodded.

"He's set up over at the far side. He's got help, I think," he replied, and Naomi smiled.

"Denke," she said, glancing around at the other stalls as she now made her way across the marketplace.

Fruit, vegetables, fish, meat, buttons, yarn, candles, bread, cakes, odds, and ends – it was all there. Naomi paused to buy a pair of knitting needles for her *mamm*, hers having snapped the evening before. It felt like the happiest of days, filled with possibility, and Naomi could not wait to see the look on David's face when she presented him with the apple fritters. They had only been stepping out for a few weeks, and whilst Naomi really knew little about him, save he was the son of Johann Glick who mended buggies on the other side of the ridge overlooking Faith's Creek, she was convinced he was the one for her. He had already told her he loved her, and she was certain a proposal was imminent.

"Perhaps even today," she thought to herself, as now she made her way along the line of stalls on the far side of the marketplace.

David's stall sold spare parts for buggies and pieces of farm equipment. He would clean up rusty old pieces of scrap and make them look like new. Naomi thought he was marvelous, and her *daed* had commented on the steadiness of such a profession.

"People always need spare parts, Naomi," he had said, which Naomi had taken as his way of endorsing David as a suitable son-in-law.

But as Naomi turned the corner by the flower stall belonging to Sylvia Raber the sight which met her filled her with horror. She shrank back, hiding behind a vase of tall sunflowers, watching David's stall. Tears rose in her eyes, her hands trembled, and it was all she could do to prevent herself from crying out in horror. David was with a woman. Naomi knew her, her name was Melinda King, and her *daed* owned a smallholding up on the ridge. They were talking, but more than talking. David was holding her hand and looking into her eyes with just the same expression he had used for Naomi.

"You look so pretty today, Melinda. It's the sunlight, it catches your eyes. That sky blue, it's so beautiful," David was saying.

Naomi, too, had blue eyes, and only the day before, David had said precisely the same thing to her as they sat by the creek eating a picnic Naomi had prepared. He had told her how pretty she was, and how he was falling in love with her.

"Oh, you don't mean that," Melinda replied, as Naomi peered through a gap in the sunflowers.

"Of course, I do. I mean every word, Melinda. I think I'm falling in love with you," David replied.

Naomi could not hold back any longer. She let out a cry, knocking the sunflowers over as she stormed forward. David turned to her in horror, his eyes wide.

"Naomi?" Melinda said in surprise, as Naomi pointed her finger at David and tears rolled down her cheeks.

"You said just the same to me. You told me my eyes caught the sunlight, and I looked pretty, and you were falling in love with me. I hate you," she exclaimed.

It seemed Melinda was as surprised to hear this as Naomi was, and she rounded on David in a show of feminine solidarity.

"You told Naomi that, too?" she asked, as David stammered.

"Well… I… I don't know. It's… I'm not…" he began, but Naomi had heard enough.

She reached into her basket, pulled out one of the apple fritters, and threw it at David, who ducked. Melinda stepped forward and cuffed him across the cheek, before turning on her heels and hurrying off across the marketplace. Bemused stallholders and customers watched the unraveling of David's affairs, and there was much tutting and shaking of heads.

"I hope you're happy – that's two hearts you've broken," Naomi exclaimed, and not wishing to waste her breath on him any longer, she turned and stormed off, fighting back the tears.

"He's not worth it," she told herself, pausing to catch her breath.

Others were looking at her, shaking their heads and whispering. Naomi felt suddenly embarrassed, even though she knew she had nothing to be ashamed of. She had done nothing wrong, and she was thankful providence had brought her to the truth before it was too late. Not wishing to be the object of other people's attention, Naomi stepped into the first store she came to. It was the ironmongers, and a smell of wood chippings and oil hit her as she entered. She looked around her, trying to appear as though she was browsing, even as she knew her composure was far from serene.

"Can I help you?" a man behind the counter asked.

He was around the same age as Naomi, with black hair and a shy look on his face. Naomi knew the ironmonger's name was Abraham Stoltzfus, but this man was not Abraham. Naomi vaguely recognized him and wondered if they had been at school together. She had never had reason to visit the ironmonger's store, and now she took a deep breath, even as her mind was still racing from the turmoil of what had just occurred.

"Oh... I was just... looking," she said.

He nodded. "I'm sharpening some tools in the back. If you need anything, just ask," he said.

He was about to turn and retreat through a door into a workshop behind, but Naomi stopped him. She was distraught, she wanted someone – anyone – to talk to about what had just happened.

"Do you know David Glick?" she blurted out, and the store assistant looked at her in surprise.

It was clear he was not used to interruptions, and now he thought for a moment and nodded.

"He comes in here sometimes. He fixes machinery, doesn't he?" he asked, and Naomi nodded.

"That's right. Have you ever seen him with women at his stall? Talking to them, I mean," she replied.

The man shook his head and looked at Naomi with a puzzled expression on his face. She knew she was talking out of turn and that he was probably embarrassed by her question. His cheeks flushed red, and he shrugged.

"I don't know. Perhaps. I just keep myself to myself back here. Did you want something?" he asked.

"I'm sorry, it's just..." she began, and now the tears welled up in her eyes and ran down her cheeks.

"Oh... don't cry. Here, my handkerchief... it's clean," he said, hurrying around the counter and handing her a neatly folded and pressed red handkerchief with white polka dots on it.

"I'm being silly. It's just... well, David and I were stepping out, courting, if you like. But I've just seen him with Melinda King, and he told her the same thing he told me. That she was pretty and had beautiful eyes and he was in love with her," Naomi stammered.

"I see. That's not very nice," the man replied, and Naomi shook her head.

There was something of a naivety about him, and an innocence she found endearing. She wiped the tears from her eyes and forced a smile onto her face.

"Well, I shouldn't let it upset me, should I?" she said, and once again, the man shrugged.

"I don't really know about such things. I'm sorry he did that, though. I'm sorry you're upset," he replied.

Naomi sighed and shook her head.

"It was only a summer romance. I shouldn't let it get to me. You've been very kind. I'm sorry to burst in on you like this, but everyone was looking at me, and... I should go home," she said, handing him back the handkerchief.

She was grateful for his kindness, but it felt like an impertinence to put on him like that, and she knew it was time she made her way home.

"Are you sure you'll be all right? You can sit for a moment. I can bring a chair from the workshop," he said.

Naomi shook her head. "*Nee, denke*, it's all right. I'll be on my way. But... would you like an apple fritter? I made them fresh this morning. They were for David, but I threw one of them at him, and..." she said, her words trailing off and feeling suddenly embarrassed at the spectacle she had made of herself.

"They're my favorite," he said.

Naomi took two out of her basket and handed them to him.

"I'll see you around," she said, and he nodded and smiled shyly at her.

Back out in the marketplace, Naomi hurried toward home. She did not look back at David's stall but thought instead of the shy, kind young man in the ironmonger's store.

When one door closes, another door opens, she thought to herself, grateful that providence had offered her comfort in her moment of sorrow and wondering if she might find a reason to return to the ironmonger's store again...

CHAPTER TWO

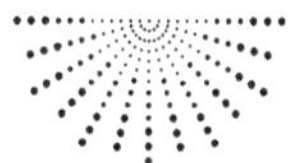

"**Y**ou've seen his true colors, Naomi. Don't go getting upset over him," Naomi's *daed*, Moses Troyer, said after she had explained to her parents what had happened in the marketplace that morning.

"Thank goodness he hadn't proposed," her *mamm*, Ruth, said, shaking her head and tutting. "You have to wonder how many other women there are, too. Can you imagine it?"

On her walk home from the market, Naomi resolved not to get upset. Her *daed* was right. She had seen David's true colors, and she was glad to know now rather than later what he was really like.

"I don't want to think about it. I got so caught up in the fantasy of it all. He was supposed to be the one. He told me he loved me. He told me I was beautiful. And then he told Melinda King that, too, and you're right, *Mamm* – how many others are there?" Naomi said, sitting herself down at the kitchen table.

Her *mamm* had cut her a piece of fruit cake and her Aunty Anna now placed a pot of coffee down in front of her.

"Drink a cup of this with sugar, and put it all behind you," she said, giving Naomi a firm look.

Naomi's aunt was her *daed's* sister, a formidable woman who had never married and lived next door but one in a row of small houses backing onto cornfields on the edge of Faith's Creek. She often took her meals with them, and was something of a second *mamm* to Naomi, and never short of a word of advice.

"But what did I do wrong?" Naomi asked because she had thought everything was going perfectly with David – how wrong she had been.

"You didn't do anything wrong. That's the problem with women in this community. They think it's up to them to do everything right. The man can do what he wants and have his pick. Don't talk to yourself like that," Anna said

Naomi nodded.

"Your aunt's right, Naomi. You didn't do anything wrong. It's him that's in the wrong. If I see him, I'll..." her *daed* began, but Naomi shook her head.

"You'll not do anything, *Daed*. I'll do what Aunt Anna says and put it behind me. There're plenty of other eligible men in Faith's Creek. I met one today in the ironmonger's store," she replied.

Her *mamm* appeared to be about to ask more about the store assistant, but it was her aunt who interrupted.

"Why this obsession with getting married, Naomi? What you need is something to take your mind off all this. Why don't you come to my quilting circle on Thursday? You know I'd like you to," she said.

Naomi knew her aunt wanted her to attend the quilting circle. She had often invited her, but Naomi had resisted. Quilting was not a skill she possessed, and whilst she was at home in the kitchen or out on the smallholding, the needle and thread had never been kind to her. She could not even sew on a button without pricking her fingers.

"I don't know... won't you get frustrated with me if I can't do it? I don't want to hold anyone back," Naomi replied, but her aunt laughed.

"Do you think that matters to anyone else that's there? Priscilla Miller is still working on the same quilt she started a year ago. If she lives long enough to finish it, they'll wrap her in it to bury her," Anna said, shaking her head and laughing.

"It would do you good, Naomi. Why don't you go?" her *mamm* said.

Naomi nodded, maybe it would be a distraction.

"All right, I will. You're right. It'll take my mind off things," she said, and her aunt beamed at her.

"That's wonderful, Naomi. I'll call for you on Thursday and you can help me set up. Now, who's for another cup of coffee?" she asked, holding up the pot.

CHAPTER THREE

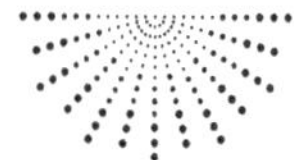

*A*aron Wittmer had been busy that day in the ironmonger's store. He had spent the morning sharpening tools and the afternoon arranging the work-shop for his employer, Abraham Stoltzfus. Tuesdays were Aaron's favorite days in the store. Abraham took a day off, and he was left in charge. But today had been different, and his predictable routine had been inter-rupted by the arrival of a young woman in distress.

The thought of her had pre-occupied him for the rest of the day. He knew her vaguely, just as he knew most people in Faith's Creek vaguely. It was that sort of place – where people knew one another, even if they did not really know one another properly. Acquaintances were two a dime, and thanks to his *mamm* and his work in the ironmonger's store, Aaron knew most people, even if his friendships were limited.

"*A strange business,*" he said to himself, as he walked home that afternoon.

He had felt sorry for Naomi – he knew she was called Naomi, Naomi Troyer. There was a year between them. Aaron was twenty-one and Naomi was twenty. They had been at school together, albeit in different classes, and Aaron remembered her as a boisterous young girl, always getting into mischief. In contrast, Aaron was shy and retiring. He liked to work with his hands and be left alone – the job at the ironmonger's store suited him perfectly.

"*I can't believe David Glick behaved like that. She's a pretty woman. He was lucky to catch her eye. It's always men like that who behave like that,*" he told himself, shaking his head and sighing.

Aaron was not good at talking to women. He could plan his words and imagine what he would say, but when it came to it, he babbled and lost his train of thought. He was nervous around women, and that nervousness had put him off seeking out their company. Aaron was happy working in the ironmonger's store and taking care of his *mamm*. There was not much time for anything more.

His *mamm* was a convalescent. There was nothing specifically wrong with her – Doctor Yoder had declared her to be as strong as an ox – but she spent her days in bed or sitting in a chair in the garden. Aaron did everything for her, but he was happy to do so, and he was looking forward to telling her about the strange events of the day.

"*Mamm*, I'm back. Are you in the garden?" he called out, as he opened the gate and walked up the path towards the porch.

He and his *mamm,* Serena lived in a small house that Aaron's *daed* had built when he and Aaron's *mamm* were first married. It was a fine dwelling, surrounded by a large vegetable garden with cut flower beds at the far end. Aaron sold the flowers and leftover vegetables at the market, whilst his *mamm* did a little sewing to bring in extra money to support them.

"I'm catching the last of the sun on the southside," came the reply, and Aaron found her sitting in the sunshine by the cabbage patch.

"Have you been all right today?" Aaron asked, leaning down to kiss her on the cheek.

His *mamm* nodded.

"I felt tired this morning, but it's always the same, isn't it?" she said, smiling up at him.

Aaron nodded. He loved his *mamm* very much, but there were times he wished she would do something – anything – to help herself. She had become used to doing nothing, and that had led to her believing she could *do* nothing.

"Did you do any sewing today?" he asked.

She shook her head. "I didn't feel like it. Why don't you sit down and tell me about your day? We don't have to eat for a while. I'm never hungry when it's hot, but perhaps you'll think of something to tempt me," she said.

Aaron sat down on the grass next to her chair.

Aaron did all the cooking, the cleaning, the gardening, the shopping, and everything that was needed around the house. It had been that way for years, and he knew his *mamm* depended on him for just about everything.

"It was a strange day," he replied

Serena looked at him in surprise. "Strange? In what way?" she asked.

"Well, you know the Troyers, don't you? The daughter, Naomi, she's about my age, and she came into the store late morning in a terrible state," he replied.

Aaron recounted the story of his encounter with Naomi and her upset at overhearing what David Glick had said to Melinda King. His *mamm* listened and shook her head.

"When will these men learn? What she needs is a nice young man, not some player like David Glick," she replied, raising her eyebrows at Aaron, who knew precisely what she was saying.

She was always dropping hints as to when he might settle down and get married. But with his job at the iron-monger's store and his duties at home, Aaron had little time to think of romance, even if his nervous disposition would allow it. He had resigned himself to a quiet life, one which was predictable and lived by a set routine. But the appearance of Naomi in the store that morning had interrupted that routine, and made him think...

"It's men like David Glick who always attract attention, *Mamm*, even if it's for the wrong reasons," he replied, shaking his head and sighing.

"Naomi Troyer... yes, I know her aunt, don't I? Anna Troyer. She's a nice woman. A little abrupt, perhaps, but that's nothing to hold against her. Well, who knows,

Naomi might come back to the store and see you," Serena said

Aaron laughed. "Why would she come back to the iron-mongers? I don't think she'll be popping in to have her tools sharpened or for a dozen nails," he said, pulling up a tuft of grass and tossing it idly into the air.

"I mean, she might come back to see *you*. Not for nails or tools, but because *you* were kind to her. Kindness counts for a lot," she said.

Aaron shook his head again. "She won't. Why would she? She's pretty and outgoing, and she could have any man she wanted. I'm just a shy counter assistant who lives with his *mamm*," he replied.

Serena tutted and said kind words, but to Aaron, what he had said was true. He saw no real qualities in himself – being kind, being gentle, being good with your hands, going to church on Sunday. Were those really the things a woman admired?

"I'll start dinner. How about I poach some eggs?" he asked, and his *mamm* nodded.

"That would be lovely, Aaron," she replied, as she sat back in the sunshine and smiled.

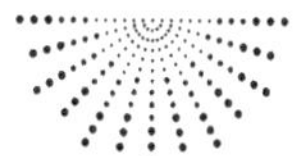

CHAPTER FOUR

"I'm not sure I want to go," Naomi said, as she sat at the kitchen table on Thursday morning eating her breakfast.

Her *mamm* looked across at her and smiled.

"You think you're not old enough to go quilting, don't you?" she said, and Naomi blushed.

"It's not that... but, well, I don't think I'll have anything in common with any of them," Naomi replied.

Secretly, she had wondered whether quilting was something a person grew into, rather than adopted at an early age. She *did* feel she was too young to be part of a glorified knitting circle. But it had been kind of her aunt to invite her, and Naomi felt she had no choice but to go.

"It's your aunt's circle, and you'll know Sarah Beiler, too," Ruth replied.

At the mention of the bishop's *fraa*, Naomi's eyes lit up. She *did* like Sarah Beiler. She liked her very much. It was she who had taught Naomi her Bible at Sunday School, and she had always made the time to speak to the *kinner* and make them feel special.

"I didn't know she went to Aunt Anna's quilting circle," Naomi replied, and her *mamm* nodded.

"She's been going for years," she replied.

Naomi smiled. It would not be so bad if Sarah Beiler was there. Naomi liked to hear her talk. She spoke with such gentle wisdom – it was always inspiring.

"But why don't you go, *Mamm*?" Naomi asked, as her *mamm* began to clear away the breakfast things.

Ruth smiled.

"I love your aunt like a sister, Naomi, but I couldn't hold my tongue if she started telling me my quilting was all wrong. Can't you imagine it?" she asked, and Naomi laughed.

She *could* imagine it. Her aunt was a delight, but she could be bossy, too, and most of the time, it was her way or the highway.

"I'd better get ready. She'll be here soon," Naomi said, glancing at the clock.

Her *daed* had already gone out to work on the small-holding at the back of the house. Naomi put on her shoes and checked her *kapp* in the mirror above the mantel-piece. She smiled at her reflection. She *was* pretty, even if David Glick told every woman in Faith's Creek the same. She liked her eyes – they were bright blue – and her nose, with its dimple. She took after her *mamm*, though her hairline was more like that of her aunt, and now she took a deep breath and resolved to put David Glick behind her.

"Ready to make a quilt?" her aunt asked, appearing on the porch a moment later and letting herself into the house.

She was part of the family and as such, she never knocked, it sometimes made Naomi jump, but not today. Naomi turned to her and smiled.

"I'm not sure about a whole one..." she began.

Anna interrupted her. "Oh, you'll be just fine. Come along now. Ruth, we're going. I'll send her back when we're finished. Don't worry about cooking tonight, I've got a casserole in I can bring over later," she called out and beckoning to Naomi, she led her out onto the porch.

It was a beautiful day – already warm, and with a clear blue sky above. Sitting inside covered in half-finished quilts was not how Naomi might have chosen to spend the day. She liked being outdoors and helping her *daed* in the vegetable patch or going for long walks by the creek. But she had promised her aunt she would come, and she knew it meant a lot to her to have at last persuaded Naomi to join the quilting circle.

"Are they there waiting for me?" she asked, and her aunt shook her head.

"They'll be here in an hour. You can help me set up," she replied.

Naomi's aunt's house was next door but one and reached by going out of one gate and through another. Their neighbor was Elijah Hochmann, an elderly man with a long white beard, who spent his days sitting on his porch reading a seemingly unending supply of books.

"*Gut* day, Anna, Naomi. Beautiful, isn't it?" he called out as they passed.

Naomi had always liked Elijah. He used to give her sweets when she was a *kinner*, and he had never been cross when her ball went over onto his grass.

"We've got the quilting circle today, Elijah. Do you want to come?" Anna called out.

Elijah laughed. "With my arthritis? I don't think so – unless you want a quilt that looks like a *kinner* made it," he replied.

Naomi gulped, what would they think of hers? She followed her aunt up her garden path and onto the porch. Her aunt's house was immaculate. Everything had its place, and Naomi always took her shoes off before going in, if she was wearing them. She wasn't today, it always felt *gut* to have her feet feel the earth beneath them.

"Now, we have coffee and cakes to share. You can hand the plates around. I'll pour the coffee. You can sit here, I'll sit here, and the others can choose," Anna said, as they let themselves into the parlor.

The chairs had been moved into a semi-circle around the stove. Naomi was thankful it was not lit, for she was already feeling warm in the heat of the day. Her aunt had pointed her to her favorite chair – a rocking chair with an embroidered cushion on the seat – and she sat down and looked around her. A box stood in the middle of the semi-circle, and her aunt opened it to reveal a dozen or so quilts, all neatly folded.

"Is this what we're going to be working on?" she asked.

Anna nodded and gave her an encouraging smile.

Naomi felt her heart stutter, what would they all think of her? What would they think when they found out she couldn't sew? This was a disaster; she shouldn't have come.

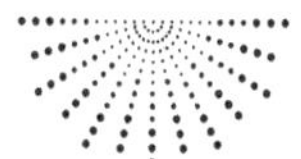

CHAPTER FIVE

"**Y**ou'll start your own. These are all works in progress. This one's mine," she said, holding up a blanket that was decorated with gold moons and stars.

It was beautiful, even as Naomi was certain she could not produce something of a similar beauty herself.

"Perhaps patchwork might be a better place for me to start," Naomi replied, and her aunt smiled.

"I'm so pleased you've come, Naomi. I've always wanted to share this with you," she replied.

Naomi was pleased, too. She loved her aunt dearly and was only too happy to be a part of something which meant so much to her, even if she was a reluctant pupil.

They spent the next hour or so getting ready. Naomi cut a large seed cake into slices, and her aunt made coffee in a large silver jug. The rich aroma filled the parlor and her aunt talked with enthusiasm about the projects they were working on, so that by the time the first knock at the door came, Naomi was actually looking forward to beginning. The first arrival was Priscilla Miller, an ancient woman who walked with a stick and a stoop, but who had a bright twinkle in her eye and greeted Naomi warmly.

"It's so nice to see a young person taking up an old craft. If we don't keep these traditions alive, they'll die out. We Amish have such a treasure trove of traditions. They're important, you know," she said, settling herself down in an armchair opposite Naomi.

"My aunt thought it would be *gut* for me to come. I've not had an easy few days," Naomi replied.

Priscilla looked at her sympathetically. "Your aunt told me. I felt so sorry for you," she said, as another knock came at the door.

This time, it was Sarah Beiler who had just arrived, and she entered the house with a smile on her face – evidently having been informed of Naomi's presence, too.

"It's so nice to see you, Naomi. I saw you in the market-place the other day. I'm sorry about what happened. These things are never easy to experience," she said, as she sat down next to Naomi.

"I'm just trying to put it behind me and not think about it too much," Naomi replied.

Sarah Beiler patted her hand. "That's the best way. And you've come to the right place to do it. We'll cheer you up, won't we, Priscilla?" she said, and Priscilla nodded.

"I always feel better after quilting. The chance to talk and spend time with a nice group of people. Here and church. That's where I like to be," she replied.

The others arrived shortly after. There was Susanna Bontrager, Rebecca Kuhns, and Mary Erb. They were all women of a certain age, but lively and sharp as any of Naomi's contemporaries. The coffee was poured, the cakes were handed around, and the women settled down to their quilting.

For a moment Naomi panicked but Sarah Beiler took it on herself to show her what to do, and to her surprise, Naomi soon found herself getting the hang of the stitching, thanks to the bishop's *fraa's* patience.

"You're getting it, Naomi, you really are," Anna said, peering over Naomi's shoulder and smiling.

"I didn't think I would. It'll take me a long time to make anything, though," Naomi replied.

"That's all right. We've got all the time in the world. We meet every week. The blankets we make go to the orphanage in Bird-in-hand. We've sent dozens over the years. You'll get there," Susanna Bontrager said, and Naomi smiled.

"I'm enjoying it," she said, never having thought she would admit as much, even as she caught her finger on the needle she was threading.

"Hold it up and press on it," Anna said, and Naomi did so, stopping the bleeding before it spoiled the quilt.

The time passed quickly, and Naomi listened as the women talked about the goings on in Faith's Creek. Between them, they knew almost everyone in the community, and it was not long before mention was made of David Glick...

"He behaved so badly towards you, Naomi. It's terrible," Mary Erb said, tutting and shaking her head.

"Well, I can't do anything about it. I've learned a lesson, and that's that," Naomi replied.

"Don't be disheartened, dear," Rebecca Kuhns said, glancing up from her quilting and smiling.

"I'll try not to be. There's *got* to be a decent man somewhere. Actually... I met one in the ironmonger's store after it happened. I was in such a state, goodness knows what he must've thought of me. He gave me his handkerchief to dry my eyes with. I felt such a fool afterward," Naomi said, thinking back in embarrassment to her encounter with the store clerk.

"Oh, that's Aaron Wittmer, Serena's son. You know him, Sarah," Mary said, glancing at the bishop's *fraa*, who nodded.

"Oh, Serena, yes. I visit her sometimes. She's always at home. She never goes out, bless her. Aaron dotes on her, but there's nothing really wrong with her. He does everything for her and has his job, too. I've always admired him. But he's painfully shy," Sarah replied, shaking her head.

Naomi realized she had not asked the man's name – though she had known him from school. Aaron Wittmer – she remembered clearly now. He had always been shy.

But she remembered him making a bird box when they were at school – it won first prize at a craft fair. It had been beautiful.

"He was nice," Naomi said, blushing under the gaze of the other women.

"We could find you a husband, Naomi. We know most of the men in this community through their *grossmammis*, don't we, ladies?" Priscilla said, and the others nodded.

Naomi laughed. They were a delightful group of women, and they had welcomed her with open arms. But as for finding her a husband... Naomi was unsure.

"We'd certainly do a better job of it than she has. It's all about choice, dear," Rebecca said, and the others agreed.

"You should invite Serena to come to the quilting circle. I've never thought of that before," Sarah said, and Mary nodded.

"I can try, or it might be better coming from you, Anna?" she said, and Naomi's aunt nodded.

"I'll happily invite her. It sounds like she could do with the company," she replied, and it seemed the matter was settled.

By the end of the morning, Naomi had completed a single square of stitching in a pattern of red and blue squares. She was proud of it, and the other women congratulated her.

"Another twenty of those and you'll have a quilt," Susannah said, in what Naomi took to be words of encouragement.

"I've really enjoyed it," Naomi replied.

Spending time with the others and learning something new had taken Naomi's mind off her troubles with David Glick. She was pleased her aunt had persuaded her to join them, and as she returned home that afternoon with the promise of her aunt's company at dinner, Naomi could only look forward to the next quilting circle and what it would bring.

CHAPTER SIX

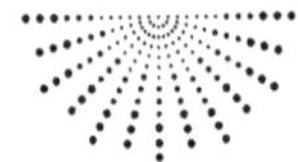

*A*aron had been busy that morning in the ironmonger's store, but Abraham had given him the afternoon off, and he was returning home to work on the henhouse he was building in the garden. Aaron planned to buy a dozen hens and sell the eggs to make some extra money. He was enterprising like that and had worked out he could recuperate his outgoing on the birds and the materials for the henhouse in just over two months if he sold the right number of eggs. He was saving up for a buggy and had already spoken to one of the local buggy builders with his ideas for the design.

"But hens first. I need some fencing, something to stop the foxes from getting in," he said to himself.

He was so preoccupied with his thoughts that at first, he did not notice Sarah Beiler sitting with his *mamm* in the garden.

"Aaron, won't you come and say hello to the bishop's *fraa?*" Serena called out, and Aaron looked up in surprise.

"Oh… I'm sorry. I didn't realize you had company, *Mamm,*" he said blushing as he turned to see Sarah smiling at him.

"Hello, Aaron. How are you?" she asked.

Aaron nodded. "I'm very well, *denke*, and yourself?" he replied.

Aaron had always liked Sarah Beiler. She was the sort of person who really listened and made time for people. Aaron often felt as though no one was interested in listening to him, but the bishop's *fraa* was different, and now he came to sit on the grass next to where she and his *mamm* were sitting by the cabbage patch.

"I've had nothing but visitors this morning. It's been lovely," Serena said, smiling at him.

"Is that right? Who else has been here?" Aaron asked.

"Anna Troyer. She came to invite me to join her quilting circle. But I'm not sure about it," she said.

Aaron glanced at Sarah Beiler. Was she here to try and persuade his *mamm* to join the quilting circle? Aaron knew it would do her *gut* to get out of the house and meet others. She spent all her time at home and rarely met with others. She had become something of a recluse, and whilst Aaron himself was not one to seek out company, he at least had his job at the ironmonger's store, which brought him into contact with all manner of different people.

"It would do you good, *Mamm*," Aaron replied.

"That's what I told her, too," Sarah said, and Serena smiled.

"Well... I used to enjoy quilting. I was quite good at it. I made you a blanket when you were a *boppli*, Aaron. I've still got it in the house in a box of keepsakes. It was green with a pattern of farmyard animals. I remember cutting them out with felt and sticking the eyes on with glue. They kept falling off. You loved it," she said.

Sarah Beiler smiled. "There you are, then. Haven't you convinced yourself? Come next Thursday and see how you like it," she said.

Aaron looked at his *mamm* and nodded. She would need further persuading, but he knew it would do her *gut*.

"Well… all right, I'll come. It might be nice. I know you and Anna and Mary," Serena said, and it seemed the matter was settled.

But later, she expressed her doubts – worrying about her state of health and whether she would be able to manage.

"I'll take you, *Mamm*. Abraham won't mind if I slip away to take you, I'll just go in early. I'll walk with you. It's not far, and I'll come and collect you, too," he said.

She smiled at him.

"You're a *gut* boy, Aaron. You've always looked after me," she said.

Aaron smiled. "Just promise you'll go. That's all," he replied.

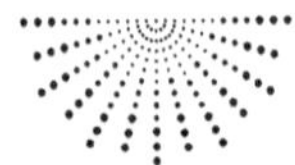

CHAPTER SEVEN

*N*aomi had just taken a tray of buttermilk chicken out of the oven. It was her *daed's* favorite and that evening, the family was celebrating his birthday. Anna was there, and she had brought a cake for dessert.

"It smells delicious, Naomi," Moses said, as she served out the buttermilk chicken on the plate.

There were buttered noodles to accompany it and mashed sweet potatoes with butter and salt.

"You've always been a *gut* cook, haven't you, Naomi?" Ruth said as Naomi sat down to join them after they had said grace.

Naomi liked to cook. It helped her to relax, and she enjoyed thinking up new recipes and ways of making old ones more interesting.

"I have. I put some dried oregano in it, and lots of pepper. Do you like it?" she asked, and her *daed* nodded.

"It's delicious. You should be proud of yourself, Naomi. I couldn't ask for a happier birthday, surrounded by my family, and with something so tasty to eat," he replied.

"And she should be proud of her quilting, too. I was looking at her stitching again this afternoon, and I can hardly believe she hadn't picked up a needle for so long. It's going to be a lovely quilt when it's finished," Anna said.

Naomi smiled. At the rate of a patch a week, it was going to take a very long time indeed to finish her blanket. But it was not the quilting Naomi had enjoyed – though it had passed the time. She had enjoyed the company of the others and learning from their wisdom.

"We'll see. I'm sure I'll finish it in the end," Naomi said, offering her *daed* more buttermilk chicken.

"We've got another new face this week. I'll have to bring an extra chair in from here if you don't mind, Ruth," Anna said.

"Who have you persuaded now? You're relentless," Moses said, laughing and shaking his head.

Anna raised her eyebrows and glanced at Naomi, who was keen to hear who this new addition was to be.

"Serena Wittmer. We talked about her the other day," Anna replied, and Naomi looked at her in surprise.

She had not taken her aunt – or the others – seriously when they had spoken of trying to find her a husband. But the invitation to Serena Wittmer was surely a nod towards Aaron. She wondered if they would try to set the two of them up together...

"Aaron's *mamm*? I thought..." she stammered, and her aunt smiled.

"It'll do her *gut*. She's a hypochondriac. She never leaves the house. It was Sarah Beiler who persuaded her. Now, Ruth, can I take one of the chairs?" she asked.

Talk turned to the practicalities, but Naomi's mind rested on what this curious invitation was meant to achieve. Was the motivation purely born out of sympathy for Serena? Was it really a matter of planting a seed? What would Aaron think if he knew Naomi's aunt, and the others, had ulterior motives?

"Well, that was a delicious meal, and I'm only glad I got to share it with my family. *Denke*, Naomi, and *denke*, sister, for the dessert, and *denke*, Ruth, for clearing everything away," Moses said after the meal had finished.

"It's not every day you turn..." Anna began, but Moses interrupted her with a fit of pretend coughing.

"That's quite enough of that," he replied, raising his eyebrows.

"I'll see you on Thursday if you're not here when I call around tomorrow," Anna said, as she bid her goodbye.

Naomi nodded, but she could not help but feel a sense of trepidation at the prospect of what was to come, or wonder what Aaron would think if he knew the truth...

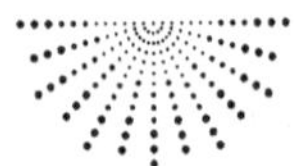

CHAPTER EIGHT

It was the day of the quilting circle, but Naomi had some chores to run before making her way to her aunt's house. She needed to buy some flour and sugar for a cake her *mamm* had asked her to make for a friend who had been ill, and Naomi had left early to walk to the grocery store. She was thankful it was not a market day and that the chances of her encountering David Glick were slim.

I don't know what I'd say to him if I met him, she thought to herself, as she made her way into the grocery store. Though her anger had faded the hurt was still there.

Having bought the flour and sugar, she emerged from the grocery store into the sunshine. It was a beautiful day, and whilst it might have been nice to spend it outside, Naomi was happy at the thought of joining the quilting circle, even as she wondered as to what her encounter with Aaron's *mamm* would bring. She was pondering this as she passed the ironmonger's, so much so that she almost bumped into Aaron, who had just emerged.

"Oh, I'm sorry," he said, stepping back with an embarrassed look on his face.

"Oh, it's all right. I wasn't looking where I was going," she replied, blushing under his gaze.

She wondered if she should mention the quilting circle but decided against it. There was no reason to do so, and he would think it odd to find out she knew his *mamm* was attending.

"Are you feeling better today?" he asked.

Naomi nodded. "Much better, *denke*. You didn't exactly see me at my best," she replied, blushing still further at the thought of having embarrassed herself.

"We're not any of us at our best at times like that. I'm sorry you had to go through that. I've not seen him since. His stall wasn't there yesterday," Aaron replied.

Naomi glanced over her shoulder at the empty market-place. She would be glad never to see David Glick again, and she was certain no woman in Faith's Creek would want anything to do with him.

"Well... it's in the past now, isn't it? Are you... busy today?" she asked, knowing full well he would be either working or taking care of his *mamm*.

"I've got a henhouse to finish. I'm getting a dozen bantams next week and they've still not got a roof over their heads. I'm going to sell the eggs," he replied.

Naomi was impressed. He was certainly good with his hands, and she could hear her *daed* complimenting him on his enterprise.

"Fresh eggs every day. How lovely," she said, and Aaron smiled.

"Something like that. Anyway, I'd better be going. I promised my *mamm* I'd help her with something today," he said, and nodding to Naomi, he hurried off across the marketplace.

Naomi wondered what it was he was doing, though she had a sneaking suspicion she could guess.

He's taking her to Aunt Anna's house, isn't he? she thought to herself, even as she realized she needed to hurry so as to arrive in time to help set up.

Naomi made her way home, dropping off the flour and sugar and bidding her parents goodbye.

"Enjoy yourself," her *mamm* said, as Naomi hurried out of the house.

"I'm sure I will," she replied, even as she wondered what the rest of the day would bring.

CHAPTER NINE

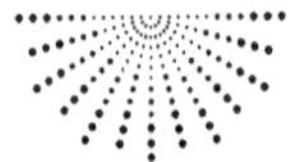

"You'll enjoy it once you get there. You know you will," Aaron said, sighing as his *mamm* now appeared to have second thoughts about the quilting circle.

"But what if I feel tired mid-way through? I don't want to be any trouble to them," she said, looking worried.

"They invited you. They want you to be there. Won't you go?" he asked, but his *mamm* looked doubtful.

"And what will we talk about? I've got nothing to say. They won't want to hear what I've got to say," she said.

"Didn't two of them come to see you? You've got lots of friends, but you don't ever make any effort with them. It's only a couple of hours, then you can come back here and I'll make us something nice to eat. How does that sound?" Aaron replied.

He did not usually insist on his *mamm* doing as she was told. But this was different. He knew it would do her good, and it would do him good, too, to have a few hours on his own. Abraham had given Aaron the rest of the day off, and he was looking forward to finishing the henhouse roof and starting a bird feeder like the one he had made at school. Aaron always had ideas for making things, even if he rarely had time to see them through.

"Well... all right," Serena replied, and Aaron breathed a sigh of relief.

Before she could change her mind, he had fetched her shawl and walking cane, and now he led her out of the garden gate and along the road towards Anna Troyer's house.

"Isn't it a beautiful day?" she said, looking across the cornfields.

"It's been a beautiful day for weeks, *Mamm*. You'd see it better if you went out once in a while," Aaron replied.

"You're too *gut* to me, Aaron. That's the problem," she said, shaking her head.

"*Nee*, I'm not. I should do more," he said, for he always felt guilty about leaving his *mamm* at home whilst he went off to work.

They were in sight of the row of three houses, the first of which Anna Troyer lived in. But as they approached, Aaron was surprised to see a now familiar figure coming toward them. It was Naomi, Anna's niece – the woman Aaron had met in the ironmonger's store and again that morning in the marketplace. What was she doing here? A young woman did not take part in a quilting circle, did she?

"Oh, hello there," she said, smiling at Aaron as his *mamm* beamed at her.

"Oh, you're Anna's niece, aren't you? How lovely. Are you coming to quilt with us?" she asked, just as the door opened, and Anna herself hurried down the steps from the porch.

"Serena, I'm so glad you could make it. And how nice to see Aaron bringing you. Naomi, this is Aaron, Serena's son, and Aaron, this is Naomi, my niece," she said.

Aaron was confused. Had Naomi mentioned nothing of their encounter in the store or was this a setup...? He smiled at Naomi, blushing under her gaze. She, too, looked somewhat bemused, but he held out her hand to him, still smiling.

"It's nice to meet you, and you, Serena," she said, turning to Aaron's *mamm*, who held out her hand and nodded, still beaming at her.

"It's so nice to meet... Aaron told me you met," she replied.

"*Mamm...*" Aaron said, hoping she would not embarrass him.

"Well, shall we go inside? We've got a lovely fruit cake made by Sarah to cut, and there's freshly brewed coffee on the stove," Anna said, taking Serena by the arm and leading her up the garden path to the porch.

Aaron and Naomi stood awkwardly by the gate.

"Do you go?" he asked, wondering whether she would be offended at the thought of a young woman attending a quilting circle.

"I do... my aunt asked me to go last week. They're all such nice women. I'm not sure you'd like it though," she replied, and he laughed.

Aaron shook his head. He could not think of anything worse than sitting around a hearth with his *mamm's* acquaintances struggling to thread a needle.

"I think I'll pass. I'd better go and finish the henhouse, and I'm making a bird box, too," he replied.

Naomi smiled. Aaron felt embarrassed. Would she think him strange for doing such things? However, he had always liked working with his hands.

"I'd like to see it when it's finished," she replied.

"Really? It's nothing special, just somewhere to put them in at night. There're plenty of foxes around. I don't want to lose them before their time," he said.

"I'm sure it'll be lovely. I'd like to see it. And the bird box. I remember you making one at school. Didn't you win a prize for it?" she asked.

Aaron could not believe Naomi had remembered such a detail from their *kinnerhood*. He *had* won a prize for his bird box – the first prize in the school craft competition. It was Bishop Beiler who had judged it, and he had commended Aaron for his craftsmanship.

"You're right. It's in one of the trees in our garden. We had some sparrows nesting in it last year. I hope we do again. I love watching them," he replied, no longer feeling embarrassed to talk about his interests, for it seemed Naomi shared those interests, too.

"I love being outdoors. I like helping my *daed* in the garden. There's always something to do, isn't there?" she said.

Aaron nodded. "Well, if you'd ever like to come and see my garden, you'd be very welcome. It's not much – I wish I had more time for it – but it's nice enough," he replied.

Naomi nodded, but just then, her aunt's voice called to her from the porch.

"Come on Naomi, we're about to cut the cake," she said, and Naomi nodded.

"Coming, Aunt Anna. Well, goodbye," she said, and with a smile, she hurried off up the garden path and onto the porch.

Aaron watched her go. She was very different now from the emotional young woman who had come bursting into the ironmonger's store the other morning.

"Goodbye," he called out, feeling confused as to what he was now feeling....

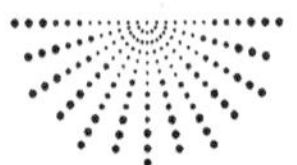

CHAPTER TEN

"Now then, Serena. If you'd like to sit here next to me, that would be just fine," Anna said, as the other women at the quilting circle took their places.

"It's lovely to have you here, Serena," Sarah Beiler said, and Serena smiled as she sat down.

"I don't get out much, as you know. It was really kind of you to invite me," she said, as Naomi poured the coffee and her aunt handed around slices of cake.

"Don't be silly. We're glad you could come," she said, settling herself down as Mary Erb opened the quilt box.

The projects were handed out, and Naomi took up her square from the previous week and began to work on it.

She felt embarrassed in front of Aaron's mamm – her quilt was nothing compared to the others.

"Naomi just started coming last week. I thought it would be *gut* for her," Anna said.

Naomi was uncertain what Aaron's *mamm* knew of her circumstances. She presumed Aaron had told her the story of their encounter in the ironmonger's – which only made the spectacle of her aunt's introduction seem even stranger. There was an elephant in the room, and Naomi was beginning to wish her aunt had not interfered.

"Oh, that's nice, and you've just started your own quilt, have you? I found one I made for Aaron when he was a baby. It was yours and Sarah's visit, Anna, that prompted it. I spent hours on it. He loved it. It's all chewed. Perhaps you'll make that one for your own *kinner*," Serena said.

Naomi smiled. She was yet to find a husband, let alone start thinking about *kinner*. But at the rate of progress she was making, it may not be her firstborn who received the blanket...

"We make blankets for orphans mainly. The poor little things don't have anything. It gives them comfort," Rebecca Kuhns said, and the others nodded.

"And it's so important to keep these crafts alive, isn't it? We don't want our precious traditions to die out," Serena said.

"And we need to guard them more than ever these days. Did you hear about the *Englischer* buying the empty store in the marketplace? He's going to turn one of them into a restaurant. Why does Faith's Creek need another restaurant?" Priscilla said, tutting and shaking her head.

Naomi had heard her *mamm* and aunt talking about the purchase of what had once been a wool store and was now lying empty. Her *daed* had called it inevitable, but her aunt had been vehemently against it.

"It shouldn't have been allowed. I don't know what Jeremiah Stubbs was thinking – letting it go to an *Englischer*. It shouldn't have been allowed," she said, shaking her head.

Naomi's *daed* had made a comment along the lines of Jeremiah Stubbs thinking more about profit than community values, but Naomi's aunt had a point. The more outsiders who moved to Faith's Creek, the more the cohesion of the community was eroded. *Englischers* simply did not understand Amish ways, nor were they interested in preserving traditions.

"It certainly doesn't need a restaurant serving Mexican food," Rebecca said, shaking her head.

"I heard it was Creole," Anna replied, tutting.

"Whatever it is, it won't do Faith's Creek any good. I won't be eating there," Mary said.

Naomi noticed Sarah Beiler was quiet. She wondered what the bishop's *fraa* thought. The polemic against outsiders was a veiled attack on him. There were those in the community who believed Bishop Beiler was too ready to welcome outsiders, and that more needed to be done to safeguard the homes and livelihoods of the inhabitants from being overrun by those who saw Faith's Creek as a pretty place to live, rather than a living, breathing community.

"Creole or Mexican, what does it matter? We're called to be welcoming to the stranger," Sarah said, looking around at the others.

Anna tutted. "You don't believe that," she said, and Sarah smiled.

"I was a stranger, and you welcomed me," she replied, quoting the scriptures.

"But that stranger didn't have an inflated bank balance and a desire to take over things," Anna retorted.

It was no use. Once Naomi's aunt's mind was made up, there could be no reneging on it, and the matter reached an impasse. On Naomi's part, she was curious as to the arrival of the *Englischer*. His name was Don Jacobs and he was coming from Florida.

"It's a long way, isn't it?" Serena said, shaking her head.

"The sunshine state. I thought most people retired there. I didn't think anyone left," Mary Erb replied.

The time had gone by quickly, and Naomi had been listening intently to the others, she had made little progress with her quilt. The next patch was half finished, but it was now time to leave.

"I've had a lovely time. But where's Aaron? I thought he'd be here by now," Serena said, rising from her chair and peering out of the window.

She looked somewhat distressed, and Naomi went over to her and put her hand on her arm.

"It's all right. I'll walk you back if you like? He's probably just absorbed in building his henhouse."

"Oh, would you really?"

"Of course, it's no trouble," she said. Naomi swallowed, would Serena think that this was done on purpose, would she mind this strange woman coming home with her? The one prone to emotional outbursts!

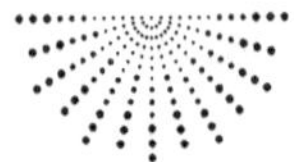

If Aaron had told his *mamm* about her emotional outburst in the ironmonger's store, Naomi wanted to ensure a more favorable impression of her was now given. Serena smiled and nodded at her offer to walk her home.

"That's very kind of you. I'd like that," she said.

Naomi glanced at her aunt, who smiled.

"Go straight home afterward, Naomi, I'll clear up here," she said, and Naomi and Serena bid the others goodbye and stepped out onto the porch.

The sun was warm on their faces as they walked across the garden and out of the gate. Naomi was not convinced Serena needed a chaperone. She walked with a stick, but it seemed more out of habit than necessity. The woman was not particularly frail and seemed quite capable.

"Did you enjoy the quilting circle?" Naomi asked, knowing how much persuasion it had taken for her to join them.

"I did. I really did. I'll be here next week, I'm sure. But I don't know if I can ask Aaron to bring me. He needs to work," she replied.

Naomi had a sudden idea.

"I'll bring you. I don't mind. I've got plenty of time on my hands. It's no trouble," she said, thinking it would be a *gut* way to prove herself reliable in the face of her previous hysterics.

Naomi was not usually given over to emotional outbursts. She was a practical sort of person, and the thought of having broken down so spectacularly in front of Aaron was embarrassing.

"You're very kind. I'd be pleased if you would," Serena replied, but just then, the figure of Aaron came hurrying towards them.

He looked anxious and out of breath and stumbled up to them, shaking his head and stammering.

"I'm... I'm sorry, *Mamm,* I got... I got so engrossed in building the henhouse, I completely forgot. Are you all right?" he asked.

"I feel a little tired, but I'm all right," Serena said, as Aaron took her arm.

"I'm sorry. I didn't mean for you to do this," he said, turning to Naomi.

But Naomi had been only too happy to help and would gladly have walked with Serena all the way back to their house.

"It was no trouble. We were having a nice conversation, in fact," she replied.

"Naomi offered to bring me next week. I've had a lovely time," Serena said.

Aaron gave a weak smile. Naomi was glad he had found the time to work on his henhouse, even as he had felt obliged to now come running. She wondered if his *mamm's* hypochondria was as much of Aaron's making as her own. He did everything for her, and she was hardly allowed to lift a finger, which in turn had made her dependent.

"That's very kind of you," he said, nodding to Naomi, who smiled.

"I'm happy to. I'm glad to help... listen, Aaron, I was wondering... might you like to go for a walk tomorrow by the creek?" Naomi asked.

She had not thought through the implications of what she was saying, only that the thought of what she was asking was pleasant. Naomi would enjoy walking with Aaron. They could sit by the water's edge, and he could tell her about the bird box he was making. But to her surprise – and sadness – he shook his head.

"I won't have time tomorrow. I've got to make up the time at the store. And I've not weeded the garden for a week. We'll have no cabbages left if I don't unchoke them," he said, as he made to lead his *mamm* towards home.

Naomi was trying hard to disguise her disappointment. She felt sad that Aaron should have refused, even as she had no reason to believe he would accept. They had made a casual acquaintance, that was all, and perhaps he was embarrassed by her forwardness.

"Oh... well, perhaps another day," she replied, and he nodded.

"I'd like that," he replied, blushing as he continued to lead his *mamm* away.

Naomi watched them go. He was so caught up in taking care of his *mamm* and working all the hours *Gott* sent. It seemed he had forgotten to take care of himself and his own needs, and Naomi felt sorry for him.

"I'll be a friend to him," Naomi resolved, even as she wondered as to her feelings over something more...

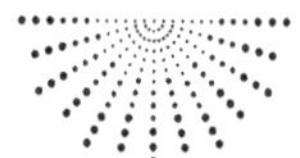

CHAPTER TWELVE

"Why don't you bake him a cake? You've got mine to make, too, don't forget," Naomi's *mamm* said when she found Naomi sitting dejectedly at the kitchen table the next morning.

She had arrived home the previous day in a low mood. She just could not understand Aaron, even as she had resolved to try her best with him. Did he not want friendship – or even something more?

"I could... I'm sorry, I forgot all about yours. I'll make them now," she replied, and Ruth smiled.

"You're an excellent baker, Naomi. Bake him a cake and take it down to the ironmonger's store. Tell him that since he didn't have time for a walk, you've come to see him, instead," she said.

Naomi nodded. It was certainly an idea, even as she was unsure of what kind of cake to bake. She had told her *mamm* the story of her attempt to spend time with Aaron, and of her confusion over his refusal. Her *mamm* had listened sympathetically and told her men were a puzzle at times – which was not overly helpful. Naomi settled on a carrot cake, pulling some fresh tops in the vegetable patch, and flavoring it with cinnamon and nutmeg. A delicious smell was soon wafting through the house, and her *daed* came in from the garden to see what was being made.

"Carrot cake? My favorite," he said, eyeing the cakes cooling on a rack.

But Naomi tapped his hand as he reached down and shook her head.

"I'm going to ice it and take it for Aaron. The other one is for *mamm's* friend. I'll make you one next time," she said, and her *daed* laughed.

"Probably for the best. My waistline seems to grow as fast as the vegetables," he replied.

When the cakes were cool, Naomi iced them with buttercream and decorated them with a dusting of cinnamon. She really was a very good baker, and both cakes looked identical and delicious.

"Cynthia's going to love that. I'll take it to her this afternoon. Poor dear, it's such a bind having a broken ankle. She can't do anything. Are you going down to the ironmonger's now?" Ruth asked.

Naomi felt suddenly nervous at the prospect of doing so. It was a kind gesture to bake a cake, but would Aaron think her odd if she just turned up out of the blue?

"I suppose I'd better," she said, taking a deep breath.

Her *mamm* smiled. "It's only a cake, Naomi. Your trouble is you invest too much. David Glick – you were set to marry him a day after he asked you out. Just slow down. Enjoy getting to know Aaron, if that's what you want," she said.

Naomi nodded.

Her *mamm* was right. She *did* rush headlong into things, and that was a recipe for getting hurt. She needed to learn from her experience with David Glick, and not make the same mistake twice. But Naomi was convinced

Aaron was different, even if she was not convinced of what it was he wanted.

"I know. It's just... well, he's a nice person. I like him," Naomi replied, admitting the feelings which had taken her quite by surprise.

She barely knew Aaron. They had met on just a handful of occasions, and never under formal circumstances. But Naomi had a feeling about him, a feeling which told her that underneath his shyness, he was a good and decent man.

"Then enjoy that," Ruth replied.

Naomi packed up the cake and put it in her basket. It was another warm day, and she wanted to get the cake to the ironmonger's store as soon as possible.

"I don't want the icing to melt before he's seen it," she thought to herself, as she hurried along the road towards the marketplace.

There was no market in Faith's Creek today, but all the stores were open, and there was a happy atmosphere about the place, with people greeting one another as they did their shopping. Naomi nodded to a couple of acquaintances and made her way to the ironmonger's store. The door was open, and she could hear raised voices coming from inside.

"I'm telling you, Mr. Jacobs, it's not for sale. I don't want to sell my store. It's been in my family for three generations, and it's promised to my son, and his son after him," Abraham Stoltzfus was saying.

Naomi peered through the window. Beyond the hanging pots and pans and tools, she could see Abraham talking to a tall man in a suit and tie. He was perhaps around thirty years of age, with a clean-shaven face and slicked-back black hair.

"Oh, come on, Mr. Stoltzfus, I'm offering you a good price. An excellent price, in fact. You can't make any money out of this place. I'll refit it, I'll make it profitable," he replied.

Abraham shook his head. "I'm not interested. No, thank you, and that's my final word on the matter."

Before the tall man could speak – and whom Naomi presumed was the same "Mr. Jacobs" the women at the quilting circle had spoken of – Naomi stepped into the store and cleared her throat. Both men turned to look at her.

"I'm sorry to interrupt. I was looking for Aaron," she said.

Abraham appeared relieved at the interruption, and he smiled but shook his head.

"You've just missed him. I sent him out to get some old newspapers at the mercantile. They had stacks of them – you wouldn't believe how many pages we get through, wrapping things and covering things," he said.

Naomi was disappointed. She had wanted to present the cake to Aaron herself, not leave it for him to find. To do so would be to create an awkward situation – he would feel the need to seek her out to thank her, and the spontaneity of the act would be gone.

"Oh. I baked him a cake, you see. It's a carrot cake, I don't want the icing to spoil in the heat," she replied.

All the while she was talking, Naomi could feel the eyes of the *Englischer* on her. It made her feel uncomfortable, and now he spoke to her.

"Baking a cake? What a talent. May I see it?" he asked.

Naomi nodded – what choice did she have but to agree? She pulled back the covering of her basket and showed the wrapped cake to the man, who nodded in approval.

"Would you keep it for him?" Naomi asked, turning to Abraham.

"I'll tell him you brought it in. He won't be long," he replied.

"*Denke*," Naomi said, and she put the basket on the counter and carefully lifted out the cake.

Don Jacobs was still looking at it admiringly.

"You could bake me one of those any time," he said, as Naomi took the basket and prepared to leave.

"Oh... well, that's very kind," she said, feeling somewhat embarrassed.

Her plan had not worked, and as she stepped out of the store, the *Englischer* followed her. He had an arrogant confidence about him, one Naomi found unsettling.

"I wanted to buy the store – I've got big plans for Faith's Creek. I've already bought the wool store. It's going to be a restaurant. I'm going to bring Tex-Mex to Faith's Creek. What do you think about that?" he asked.

Naomi froze, would he not leave her alone?

CHAPTER THIRTEEN

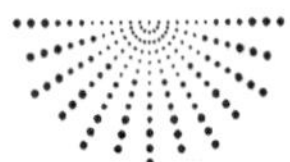

*N*aomi did not like to tell him precisely what she thought of that, and she could only imagine what her aunt would have said if she had been there to answer. Faith's Creek already had a café, and it certainly did not need a restaurant like that.

"Oh... I'm sure I don't know," she replied, trying to remain diplomatic as she tried to sidle away from him.

"That's right – Tex-Mex there, pizza here, and fried chicken over there," he said, pointing to different parts of the marketplace.

He spoke as though the deal was done, even as Naomi knew that many in the community would object.

"It sounds... lovely," she replied, and he smiled.

"It'll really bring this place along. Who needs a wool shop and an ironmonger's store these days? Progress, that's what it is," he said.

He had not even bothered to ask her name or ascertain anything about her. But Naomi had seen enough of him to know just what sort of man he was. If her aunt had made sweeping statements about *Englischers*, then this man was the embodiment of the stereotype, and whilst Naomi knew not all outsiders were the same, this one certainly lived up to the expectation.

"My aunt runs a quilting circle. They need the wool for their projects. They make blankets for the orphanage in Bird-in-hand," Naomi said.

"Isn't that super? I'm sure orphans need blankets. Doesn't the government provide them?" he asked.

"Well..." Naomi began, but he interrupted her.

"But listen to me, talking about blankets ... I haven't introduced myself, Don Jacobs. I've come up from Florida. I own a few motels and a golf course down there. But it's so difficult to start something new there. It's all been done. But here... yes, a place like this... it's all here just waiting," he said.

Naomi sighed; he wasn't listening to the locals. "I'm Naomi," she replied, though it seemed he had little interest in her, and only what he might gain by association.

"It's a pleasure to meet you. You'll be seeing a lot more of me around here, that's for sure. Say... why don't we have dinner together? Yes, we should. You can tell me all about Faith's Creek – I need to know more about it if I'm going to buy it," Don said, laughing.

Naomi was trying desperately to think of an excuse, but he was the sort of man who would not take no for an answer.

"Well... I," she began, and he nodded and put his hand on her shoulder.

"That's settled then. We can go to the café across the marketplace. It doesn't look like much, but it'll soon be gone. Once I've opened my restaurant, no one's going to want to eat there anymore. Tomorrow night at seven o'clock. I'll meet you there. What did you say your name was again?" he asked, laughing as he spoke.

"Naomi, Naomi Troyer," she replied.

"Troyer – all right, I'll look you up. See you then. I've got so much to do and so little time to do it in," he said, and with a swagger, he marched off across the marketplace, answering his mobile phone as he went.

Naomi sighed.

"What have I done?" she thought to herself, as she made her way dejectedly home.

Aaron was watching from the doorway of the ironmonger's store. He had returned with the newspapers a short while before, and Abraham had shown him the cake Naomi had baked for him. Carrot cake was his favorite, and Abraham had told him he might catch Naomi in the marketplace and thank her. He had hurried outside, but as he had done so, he had caught sight of Naomi talking to the *Englischer* whom his employer had also mentioned.

"He wanted to buy the store. Can you imagine it?" Abraham had said, tutting and shaking his head.

But it was not the *Englishcher's* arrogant words about buying the ironmonger's store that most upset Aaron, but what he heard as he emerged from the door. Naomi was agreeing to have dinner with the man who was laughing about the closure of the café. Aaron could not believe it. Was Naomi really interested in him?

"Seven o'clock tomorrow," the *Englischer* called out, as he answered his mobile phone.

"I'll see you then," Naomi replied, as she hurried away.

Aaron sighed. He had been a fool to think Naomi was interested in him, and he cursed himself for refusing to walk with her by the creek that day.

I should've said jah. She moves on pretty quickly, he thought to himself, his appetite for cake now diminished...

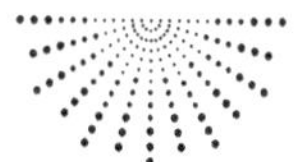

CHAPTER FOURTEEN

"I've been such a fool to stay in the house like this for so long. I could've been going to the quilting circles for years," Serena said.

"No one stopped you," Aaron replied, rolling his eyes

They were in the kitchen and Serena was sitting at the kitchen table whilst Aaron made buttered noodles for dinner. The cake Naomi had made stood on the side, still uncut.

"And it was so nice to meet Naomi. Isn't she lovely? She's promised to take me next week. And making you that cake, wasn't it a kind gesture? She must really like you. Don't you like her?" Serena asked.

Aaron sighed. He *did* like Naomi, but he had felt hurt by her acceptance of Don Jacobs' invitation to dinner. A woman did not just accept an invitation to dinner unless there was something behind it – or so Aaron thought. But he could not understand what it was about the *Englischer* she found attractive. He was an arrogant man, and half a dozen people had come into the store that afternoon complaining about him. It seemed he was determined to buy up the whole of Faith's Creek, and whilst Abraham had refused, it seemed others had been tempted.

"I do, but... she's having dinner with that *Englischer*. I heard her agree to it today. I should've gone for a walk with her when she asked me to. But I didn't know what to do. I had to go to work, and I've got too many chores to do here," Aaron said, shaking his head.

"Oh, Aaron... I realized something after the quilting circle," Serena said, as Aaron served out the buttered noodles.

"What's that?" he asked, sitting down opposite her.

His *mamm* took up her fork and smiled at him.

"I can do things myself. I got so caught up in thinking I was helpless that I made myself helpless. I've held you back, Aaron," she said, reaching across the table and putting her hand on his arm.

"*Mamm, nee*, you've not held me back..." Aaron replied, but his *mamm* interrupted him.

"I have, Aaron. You felt you couldn't go for a walk with Naomi because you needed to look after me. But that's not true. I can take care of myself. And I should be taking care of you. Don't hold back on my account and don't think you can't do things because of me. I'd feel terrible if that was the case," she replied.

Aaron gave a weak smile. He would never admit it, but his *mamm* was right. He did feel held back, and whilst he would never resent her, there were times he resented his circumstances. He wished he had the confidence of men like David Glick and Don Jacobs – men who seemed to get anything they wanted and with a minimum of effort.

"But it's too late now. She's made her choice. She's going to have dinner with that *Englischer*," Aaron said, sighing at the thought of having missed his chance.

The strength of his feelings had taken him by surprise. He had not intended to fall for Naomi, but her wit and charm, her pretty face, and her kindness had all given rise to unexpected feelings in him. He wished he could have more confidence, even as he knew it would not do him any good now.

"And is that it? Are you just going to give up?" she asked.

Aron shrugged. He did not know what to do. Was it not a losing battle? He wondered about the cake, and what it had meant? Was it just a thank you for lending Naomi his handkerchief in her hour of need, or did it mean something more?

"Well... but I don't know what to do. What should I do?" he asked.

Serena smiled. "Having dinner with a man doesn't mean anything. She asked you to go for a walk with her, didn't she? Well, why don't you say *jah*?" she said.

Aaron looked at her with a puzzled expression on his face. Could he just jump in like that as though nothing had happened? Then there was Don Jacobs, too. Aaron did not know what the other man would do if he felt threatened. It was all so complicated, and Aaron wished he had just stuck to building henhouses...

"I suppose I could. But would she accept? I just feel like I've burned my bridges," Aaron replied, pushing aside his plate.

But his *mamm* shook her head. "She's a nice young woman. She's already proved that – offering to take me to the quilting circle and baking you a cake – and I'm sure she'll say *jah*. You'll only know if you try," she replied.

But it was trying, which was the issue. Aaron did not know if he could summon the courage to do so. What if Naomi was the one to reject him after his foolish snub? He did not know what to do, even as he knew what he would have liked to do had he been a man like David Glick or Don Jacobs. But Aaron was nothing like those men, and whilst he wanted only to be himself, he wondered if he would ever find happiness being so...

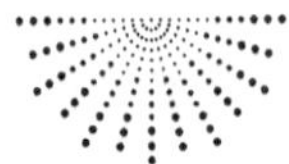

aomi was feeling miserable. Her plan had been a disaster, and it had resulted only in a most unexpected – and unwelcome – outcome. She did not know why she had said yes to Don Jacobs' invitation. She had barely spoken two words to him, but it was he – not she – who had made the decision to have dinner together, a dinner she was dreading more and more with every passing moment.

"I shouldn't have said *jah*, but he just... I couldn't say *nee*," she exclaimed shaking her head as she sat at the kitchen table that evening.

Her aunt was having dinner with them, and she had made her views on the matter very clear indeed.

"You could've said *nee*. You could've told him you weren't interested. Why did you agree to it?" her aunt asked, shaking her head.

"Oh... I don't know. He told me he was buying this and that, then the next moment we were due to have dinner together," Naomi replied.

It seemed so foolish when she put it like that. But that was how it had happened. Naomi had not so much agreed, as had been scheduled in. She wondered if all *Englischers* were like this. If they were, she was glad she did not know any others.

"Buying this and that? Oh, that's terrible. How dare he come here and make such demands," Anna said, and she banged her fist on the table.

"Now, Anna, don't get upset. It's not Naomi's fault he's causing trouble," Moses said, though he, too, had expressed his concerns.

Her *mamm* tutted.

"And what about Aaron? Don't you think he might be feeling a little upset by all this?" she asked.

Naomi nodded. She did not know if Aaron knew about the dinner with Don Jacobs. She had heard nothing from him about the cake, nor had he sought her out to agree to the walk she had suggested. But if he did know she was having dinner with the *Englischer*, he was bound to feel hurt by it. He would be confused why she should bake him a cake and suggest a walk when it seemed her intention was to court the favors of an outsider. It was all a terrible mess.

"He'll be feeling hurt, and his poor *mamm*, too," Anna said.

She was not holding back, and tears welled up in Naomi's eyes as she rose from the table. "I didn't mean to. I like Aaron. I don't want to hurt him," she exclaimed.

"Oh, Naomi, don't get upset," Ruth said, rising to her feet and putting her arm around Naomi's shoulders.

"Now look what you've done, Anna," Moses said, but her aunt only shrugged her shoulders.

"You know my opinion on *Englischers*, Moses," she said, and Moses rolled his eyes.

But Naomi had heard enough. She was angry with herself for accepting Don Jacobs' invitation, even as she knew there was nothing she could do about it. She would have to meet him for dinner and suffer the consequences. If Aaron found out, he would think she was no better than David Glick – playing one person off against another, even if that was far from the truth...

"I didn't mean to upset him. I really like him. What can I do, *Mamm*?" Naomi asked as she sobbed into her *mamm's* shoulder.

Ruth sighed. "Trust in *Gott*, Naomi. That's all you can do," she replied, as Naomi clung to her.

Naomi wanted to trust in *Gott*. She wanted to believe there was something better for her. But her mind was so filled with doubts, and she wondered if she had already burned her bridges with Aaron, even before anything more could come of their fledgling friendship.

"I'll try," she whispered, even as fresh tears rolled down her cheeks.

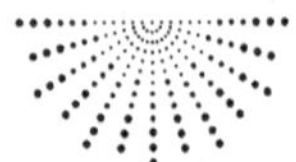

aomi was looking at her reflection in the mirror. She had chosen a plain blue dress and a darker blue shawl to wear. Her *kapp* was as always on her head and she had combed her hair and plaited it on beneath it.

"Are you ready, Naomi? It's nearly time. I'll drive you in the buggy," Moses called out.

Naomi took a deep breath and rose to her feet. "I'm coming, *Daed,*" she replied, resolved now to accept her fate.

There was nothing Naomi could do but go along with the plan for the evening. She would meet Don Jacobs and the two of them would have dinner. That would be it. She would not see him again. It was an experience to be endured, rather than savored.

"You look very pretty," her *daed* said, as they made their way out to the buggy.

"But I don't want to impress him. I don't want anything to do with him," she replied, shaking her head.

Her *daed* turned to her with a sympathetic look in his eyes.

"Don't let your aunt tell you what to do. If you want to have dinner with this man, then have dinner with him," he said, rolling his eyes.

"But I don't... well, I agreed to it, I know, but... oh, I feel such a fool," she exclaimed, and her *daed* smiled.

"Come on, Naomi. Let's go," he said, clambering into the buggy.

Naomi climbed in next to him and they set off for the marketplace. Naomi could only imagine what her acquaintances would say if they saw her having dinner with Don Jacobs. She would be ostracized and called a traitor. She was not looking forward to the quilting circle, knowing her aunt's friends would not hold back their opinions.

"He's waiting for me," she said, as they pulled into the marketplace.

Her *daed* smiled and leaned over to kiss her on the cheek.

"Shall I pick you up later?" he asked, but Naomi shook her head.

"No, *denke*, I'll walk. I'll need some fresh air after all the hot air," she replied, climbing down from the buggy.

Don came to meet her. He was wearing a suit and tie, his hair was slicked back, and he greeted her with a flashing smile.

"Did you really come in that?" he asked, pointing at the buggy as Naomi's *daed* drove away.

"Well, my *daed* wanted to drive me. We use the buggies every day," she replied.

Don laughed. "You should get a car – most people have them, you know," he said, in a patronizing tone.

Naomi had never thought about the buggies as anything but the most efficient form of transportation. They were fast and convenient, and she had always loved taking care of the horse, whose name was Flash. It was clear

Don Jacobs understood nothing of the Amish way of life, nor was he willing to learn about it.

"I prefer the buggy," she replied, as they walked towards the café.

"They'll soon be obsolete. I'm thinking of opening a garage in Faith's Creek. You've got wide open roads here, they're perfect for RVs," he said, opening the café door for her. "If I sold RVs I could make a killing, everyone would want one."

Naomi sighed. This was going to be a long evening...

"I made my first $100 selling lemonade on the sidewalk. I took that and invested it in a bigger, juicer lemonade stand and then I sold more, and that was the start of my first business. I had lemonade stands across the town – I had my friends from school franchise them from me," Don said after they had finished their main course.

"That sounds... very interesting," Naomi replied, though she was feeling thoroughly bored. All he talked about was himself and how he was successful.

Don had talked of little but himself since they had sat down – apart from complaining loudly about the range of food on offer.

"I can't eat this – shoofly pie? Buttered noodles? Boiled chicken? This place is crying out for some decent food. Where's the pizza? The ribs? The burgers? Don't you people even have a diner?" he had exclaimed, and the astonished waitress had mumbled something about tradition.

But over the course of the evening, it became clear that he was not interested in tradition. Don Jacobs intended to sweep away tradition and establish something new. A restaurant was just the start. He had three planned, not to mention the garage, and a store on the edge of Faith's Creek selling just about everything imaginable.

"And how soon do you plan on doing all this?" Naomi asked as the waitress brought them the dessert menu. Her fear was growing, could he really change so much about the home she loved?

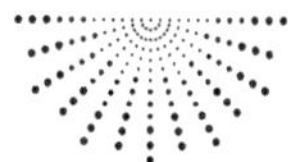

"As soon as possible," Don said. "I'm just waiting for finance. That's why I'm trying to get as many people on my side as possible. I want firm acceptances of my offers, then I'll be in a position to purchase the property straight away."

Naomi nodded. She did not like the sound of his plans She could hear her aunt's words ringing in her ears. They would call her a traitor, even as she would rather have been anywhere but there.

"But it's not certain?" she asked.

Don laughed. "Nothing's certain in business. That's the first rule. But I've got a good feeling about it. You need these things here. You need Don Jacobs. Now, what have we got here...? Apple pie, I suppose you can't go wrong with apple pie. Waitress, two apple pies, and make mine with heavy cream on the side," he called out.

Naomi was resigned to another course, even as she would much rather have gone home. The waitress brought their desserts, glancing at Naomi with a withering look. Everyone in the café was watching them, and Naomi knew that word of her betrayal would soon spread.

"And you'll move to Faith's Creek, will you?" she asked.

Don Jacobs laughed. "Move here? I'll buy a house, but I won't stick around much. I've got my villa in Florida, and an apartment in New York City. I can't see myself spending much time in this backwater place. I'm surprised anyone stays here at all – what opportunities are there? It's tourists you want. Bring them in, show them a few crafts, and make them feel they've experienced the Amish way of life. Yes, that's it, I could open a visitor center," he said, as he dug a fork into his piece of apple pie.

Naomi had never heard anything like it. He had no understanding – or interest – in their way of life, nor was he willing to learn. Faith's Creek was simply a cash cow. He was like a prospector of old, seeking out fresh seams of gold and mining them for profit. It made her feel sick to think of how he viewed their way of life. Faith's Creek was not a museum, it was a living, breathing community, and far from being backward, its residents looked to the future with confidence in their traditions.

"I'm sure you'd get lots of people to come," she replied, pushing aside her plate.

"There's so much potential here. It just needs someone with a vision. That's where I come in," he said, calling for the check.

Don Jacobs' one redeeming feature was the fact that he paid for dinner. But like anything, it came at a price.

"You're very kind," Naomi said, as they got up to leave.

"Not at all. You've told me a lot about Faith's Creek. You could be a real asset to me. I'd happily look to employ you in some capacity. You could be my agent here. Let's meet again tomorrow," he said, as he ushered her out of the café.

Naomi knew she had to be firm, but once again, Don was taking over.

"Well, I'm not sure about tomorrow. I've got chores to see to at home," she said, but he only waved his hand dismissively.

"The day after tomorrow, then. And what chores can you have? Baking? Feeding chickens? What do you people do all day?" he asked.

Naomi did a lot. She cooked, she gardened, she saw to the hens, she mended and sewed, but in Don Jacobs' eyes, it seemed this was not enough. Business – that was what Don Jacobs valued. Making money, being busy. There was no time in Don Jacobs' world for spending time on things that, whilst not making a profit or advancing gain, really mattered.

"We find plenty to fill our time with," she replied, wondering if the *Englischer* had ever paused to wonder if there was more to life than "business."

"I'm sure I could fill it better. I'll look you up in the next few days. We'll come to an arrangement," he said, as they parted ways outside the café.

Naomi nodded. It was the last thing she wanted, but once again, she had found it impossible to say what she meant. Sighing to herself, Naomi turned to walk home. It was getting late, and dusk was falling. She was surprised to see a lamp burning in the ironmonger's store, and she wondered if Aaron was working late. For a moment, Naomi paused, wondering if she should step inside and speak to him. But it hardly seemed fair. She had already put on him with her problems, and to do so again seemed unfair. This was something she had to deal with herself, for she knew how hurt Aaron would be if he knew the truth.

"We were just getting to know one another. Things always get spoiled," she thought to herself, as she made her way dejectedly home.

Aaron *was* working late. He was sharpening tools in the workshop behind the ironmonger's, and having finished up, he was preparing to go home. His mind was filled with thoughts of Naomi, even as he realized how foolish it was to think of her. She had made her choice, and her choice was the *Englischer*.

"And there's nothing you can do about that," he told himself, as he closed up the store and stepped out onto the marketplace.

But as he was locking up, he heard the sound of a now familiar voice. It was Don Jacobs, and he was speaking loudly into a cell phone.

"... that's right, I've found someone. She's a naïve sort – they all are around here. But if I get her on my side, we're in. I'm going to give her a job, make her feel like I think she's important. She'll persuade them. A restaurant first, then a visitor center, a garage, too... what's that? Oh, her name is Naomi or something. It doesn't matter. I've got her wrapped around my little finger."

Aaron's eyes grew wide with horror. Don Jacobs had no intention of courting Naomi; she was merely a pawn in his game. He watched as the *Englischer* walked away, still talking on his cell phone, and arrogantly suggesting it would not be long before Faith's Creek was his.

Aaron shook his head. He did not know what to do to stop Don Jacobs, but one thing was certain, Naomi needed to know the truth...

CHAPTER EIGHTEEN

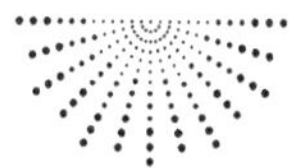

*N*aomi felt even more dejected than before. It was the day of the quilting circle, and her aunt had informed her that Aaron's *mamm* would be making her own way there that day.

"Didn't she want me to pick her up?" Naomi asked, as she and her aunt prepared the parlor and made coffee, but Anna shook her head.

"*Nee*, she didn't, and I don't blame her. Fraternizing with *Englischers*. Everyone's talking about you, Naomi. When I went to the market earlier on, I heard them. You and the *Englischer* dining together at the café... the way he talks, it's like he's already bought the whole community. He wants to turn us into a museum and put us all on show. How can you want anything to do with him?" she demanded.

Naomi sighed. She knew what was being said about her. It was inevitable. But it was not the truth. She detested Don Jacobs, even as he had swept her along in his plans.

"It's not like that, Aunt Anna. I don't want anything to do with him," she replied, and her aunt tutted.

"Then why did you have dinner with him? Why did you agree to see him again? He offered you a job, didn't he?" she demanded.

Naomi rolled her eyes. Her aunt was well informed, and Naomi knew there was no shortage of people in Faith's Creek willing to pass on their information.

"I didn't agree to see him again. I left it open. And *jah*, he offered me a job, a job I don't want. I'm not going to see him again, not if I can help it," she replied.

"You don't seem to be making much of an effort to resist. Take charge of your own destiny, Naomi. If you want to court this man, then so be it, but don't expect the rest of us to support you," Anna said, just as a knock came at the door.

Naomi was despairing. Her aunt simply would not listen, and she could only imagine what the rest of the quilting circle would say. The refusal of Aaron's *mamm* to allow Naomi to collect her that day was proof enough that Aaron knew all about her and Don Jacobs. She wondered what he must think of her – something awful, she reasoned – and she felt thoroughly dejected at the thought of having spoiled the chance of something more between them. But she was relieved at the sight of Sarah Beiler arriving first – the bishop's *fraa* never judged anyone, and Naomi knew she would find a kind word in her, even if the rest of the group shunned her.

"Hello, Naomi. How are you?" Sarah asked as she sat down in her usual chair.

"I've been better," Naomi replied, glancing at her aunt, who shook her head.

Sarah smiled sympathetically. Naomi knew she knew. Everyone knew.

"Don't let these things get you down, Naomi. They'll pass," she replied, even as Naomi wondered if they ever would...

Next to arrive was Priscilla, followed by Rebecca, Susanna, and Mary. They greeted Naomi curtly, settling themselves down without the usual chatter.

"Is Serena coming?" Priscilla asked.

"I think so," Anna replied.

A few moments later, with silence reigning, a knock came at the door. Naomi rose to answer it, the atmosphere feeling as though it could be cut with a knife. It was Serena, and she nodded to Naomi without a word.

"I'm glad you could make it," Naomi said, as Serena stepped inside.

"Coffee, Serena?" Anna asked, and Serena nodded and sat down.

"Well, I think it's terrible. He was in every store in Faith's Creek offering to buy it," Mary said, breaking the silence.

Everyone knew to whom she was referring, and the others shook their heads.

"These outsiders, coming here and thinking they can take over. He's from Florida, or so they say. He wants to open a restaurant, a garage, and a visitor center. Can you imagine it? It'll rip the heart and soul out of this community. We can't allow it," Rebecca said, and the others agreed.

It felt like a personal attack on Naomi. It *was* a personal attack on her. In the eyes of the community, Naomi had become a bedfellow with the *Englischer,* and that was unforgivable.

"We have to see what happens. I'm not sure it'll come to that," Sarah Beiler replied, and Naomi was grateful to her for taking a stance.

But now it was Serena who spoke up.

"It might not do. But it doesn't help when certain members of the community take it on themselves to fraternize with the enemy. There're plenty of *gut* men in Faith's Creek, but there are some who can't see that," she said.

Naomi knew precisely to whom her words were directed.

Her lip trembled, and she felt tears welling up in her eyes. She had done nothing wrong, but here she was, being blamed for all the problems caused by the *Englis-*

cher. Her aunt said nothing in her defense, and Naomi tossed her patchwork aside and rose to her feet.

"It's not like that. It's not like that at all," she exclaimed, and the other women looked at her in surprise.

"Naomi... don't make a scene," Anna said, but Naomi had heard enough.

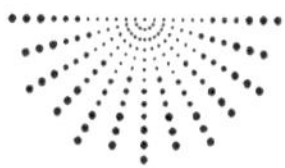

CHAPTER NINETEEN

Why were they blaming Naomi when she had simply been manipulated? "I didn't want anything to do with him. I *don't* want anything to do with him. You're all wrong," Naomi said, and before anyone could say anything more, she stormed out of her aunt's house, slamming the door behind her and hurrying down the steps.

Tears rolled down her cheeks, and she paused at the gate, leaning on it to catch her breath.

"Why won't they understand? Why can't they see it?" she asked herself.

But the answer was clear enough. People saw what they wanted to see, and Naomi had become the scapegoat for

Don Jacobs and the ills he had brought to the community of Faith's Creek. It was a terrible indictment, but one Naomi knew she would have to live with. She sighed and shook her head, not wishing to go home, but not wishing to return to the quilting circle.

Her aunt would be angry with her for storming out, but Naomi did not care. She wanted her and the other women to know they had upset her, and now she wished she had never agreed to attend the quilting circle in the first place.

"It was all a mistake," she exclaimed to herself, but there was nothing she could do to persuade the community otherwise.

She decided to go for a walk and clear her head. It was another beautiful day. They had seen no rain in weeks, and everywhere was dry. She would walk by the creek and sit in her favorite spot by the water's edge. It was a good place for thinking, and Naomi knew she had a lot of thinking to do. But as she stepped out of the gate, she was horrified to see a familiar figure coming toward her. It was Don Jacobs, and when he saw her, he called out to her.

"Oh, there you are. I asked one of the storekeepers, and he told me you lived up here. It's a quaint place," he said, coming to meet her.

Naomi was rooted to the spot. She wanted to flee, but there was nowhere to run. If the women at the quilting circle saw her with him, it would only serve to confirm further what they believed to be the case.

"Oh... I... I've got to be..." she began, trying desperately to think of an excuse to rebut him.

"I was hoping I'd find you. I've got a meeting about the restaurant. You can come with me. I need someone who knows the lie of the land. Someone who knows the community. There're a lot of people against it. I don't understand why. I've never known such hostility to progress. You can tell them why it's a good idea," he said, and now he came right up to Naomi and took her by the arm.

"I don't think so. I don't have time right now," she stammered, and he looked at her and rolled his eyes.

"What could you possibly be doing instead? Come on," he said, but at that moment, another voice interrupted him.

It was Aaron, who had just appeared around the corner.

"Naomi? Are you all right?" he asked.

Naomi blushed. She did not want Aaron to see her with Don Jacobs. It would only serve to confirm what she was certain he already believed.

"She's quite all right. She's coming with me," Don Jacobs replied.

"I'm not," Naomi replied, shaking his hand off her arm.

Don's eyes narrowed, and he glanced back at Aaron and shook his head.

"You can't possibly see anything in him. He's just a boy," he said, smirking.

Naomi was speechless. To see the two of them standing side by side was such a contrast – the arrogant businessman and the sweet, kindly store assistant. Once again, her eyes filled with tears, and she shook her head, overcome with emotion at what was occurring.

"I..." she stammered, but Aaron interrupted him.

"This 'boy,' knows all about you, Don Jacobs. I heard what you said about Naomi," he replied, and the look on Don Jacobs' face changed.

Naomi, too, stared at him with wide-eyed amazement.

"What... what do you mean, Aaron?" she asked.

Aaron took a deep breath. "After the two of you had dinner... I heard him on his cell phone. He was talking about you to someone. He was saying you were naïve, and that he was going to use you to further his plans for Faith's Creek. It was all worked out, or so it seemed," he said.

Don made an angry sound. "Lies. You're talking nonsense," he said, but Naomi knew Aaron would never tell a lie.

His words were the truth. She rounded on Don Jacobs and pointed her finger at him, finally summoning the words she had wanted to say all along.

"I don't want anything to do with you. I never wanted anything to do with you. I can see you're just using me for whatever ends you think you're bringing to this community. But we don't want it or you. Do you hear me? We don't want a restaurant, or a garage with RVs, or a visitor center, or whatever other awful things you're planning. We want our community to stay just as it is. It's perfect, and it doesn't need to change. Progress isn't always forward. Sometimes, it's about preserving what's already as good as it can be," she exclaimed.

Don seemed taken aback at these words, as though no one had ever spoken to him in such a way before. He glanced at Aaron, who stepped forward to stand next to Naomi.

"It's true. We don't want it. We like our way of life. You might call it simple. We call it freeing. We don't need the trappings of the modern world; we've got everything we need right here. If you try and change that, you'll soon see we're not backward, we know what we want, and this is it," he said.

Naomi nodded. She felt proud of Aaron for standing up to Don Jacobs and for defending her. She had no doubt he was telling the truth, and now the two of them stood side by side as Don shook his head.

"I should've known... you people don't want what's good for you. I don't know why I came here in the first place," he exclaimed.

"To make money," Naomi replied.

The *Englischer* sneered. "Money that could've been yours. All of you. Well, I'm done with this place," he said, and turning on his heels, he marched off down the road, muttering under his breath.

Naomi breathed a sigh of relief and turned to Aaron who gave a weak smile.

"I'm so sorry, Aaron," she said, as tears rolled down her cheeks, but would he and the rest of the district ever forgive her?

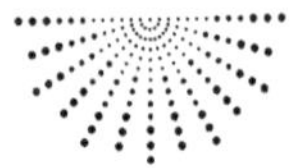

aron was not sure what had emboldened him to speak up in Naomi's defense. He had been coming to collect his *mamm* from the quilting circle, but the sight of Don Jacobs and Naomi had made his blood boil. He was so angry at the way the *Englischer* had treated her, even as he was uncertain why she had allowed herself to be so treated.

"Why did you let him behave like that?" he asked, as they watched Don disappear around the corner.

Naomi brushed the tears from her eyes and shook her head.

"It wasn't like that. I didn't mean for you to get the wrong impression, Aaron. You must think terribly of me," she said.

Aaron had to admit his thoughts had veered in that direction, even as his feelings had remained the same. He liked her. More than that, those feelings were growing stronger by the moment. But the sight of her with Don Jacobs and the knowledge of what she had done had upset him terribly. It felt like a betrayal – not only of him but of the entire community.

"I... well, what happened?" he asked.

Naomi shook her head and sighed.

"He didn't let me speak. He didn't let me get a word in edgeways. But I didn't know the extent of it. I didn't know what you'd overheard. He had a way of... well, sweeping me along with him. I know what he was doing now, though. He just wanted me to be his stooge. I wasn't going to go along with it, but he had such a forceful personality. I couldn't stop him; I was just being polite and it all got out of hand. I'm so sorry, I didn't mean to hurt you if you were hurt..." she said, and it seemed she was astonished at how easily she had been led along by the *Englischer*, who it was clear had only wanted to use her for his own ends.

Aaron shook his head. He felt sorry for Naomi. She had been used as a pawn in a game, and it would only have been a matter of time before Don Jacobs cast her aside. But he believed her, and he could see the sorrow and regret etched on her face. She looked at him with tear-filled eyes, and Aaron knew the time had come for forgiveness.

"I was... hurt... I didn't understand. There was the cake, and the next moment, you were going for dinner with him, and then I heard what others were saying, about how you'd agreed to help him. I know I shouldn't have listened to gossip, but it was all too much," he replied.

Aaron had lived a sheltered life, and the events and reve-lations of the past few days had come as something of a shock. But now his mind was clear, and he was certain Naomi was telling the truth.

"I don't blame you for listening. It was only natural but it was not true. I baked the cake as a thank you, but also... well, I was upset you didn't want to go for a walk by the creek. I wanted you to know... how I was feeling," she replied.

Her words caused Aaron's stomach to knot. He did not know what she meant by feeling... even as he hoped it was the same feeling he was experiencing.

"It was a delicious cake," he replied.

Naomi smiled.

"They tried to set us up, didn't they," she said, glancing back towards her aunt's house, and Aaron smiled.

His *mamm* had made her feelings about Naomi clear – both good and bad. She had told him how angry she was at hearing Naomi had fraternized with the *Englischer*, but before that, she had told him how happy she was that he and Naomi were getting to know one another. She wanted him to be happy, and it seemed the rest of the quilting circle had had the same intention.

"They did, and I suppose they managed it, in a round-about sort of way," he replied.

"But is it what you want?" Naomi asked, and Aaron took a deep breath...

Naomi had been shocked by the appearance of Aaron but was thankful for his intervention. He had saved her from certain disaster, for she was not certain she could have overcome the *Englishcher's* forceful personality alone. But now she waited with bated breath for Aaron's response. Did he want the same as her? And could there be something more between them? The past few days had created such a mess, and Naomi only wanted the chance for a fresh start and something new.

"If it's what you want, too," he replied.

Naomi breathed a sigh of relief.

"It is. It's just what I want. I want to forget all about Don Jacobs and how close I came to disaster. I want to wipe the slate clean. I didn't want anything to do with him, Aaron. It was you I wanted to get to know. I know it was a chance encounter that brought us together, but doesn't that mean something? Isn't that the hand of fate? *Gott's* providence," she asked.

Aaron nodded. "I never expected to find someone. I thought it was hopeless. But... well, you're right, *Gott* certainly had a hand in it. Would you like to start again?" he asked.

Naomi nodded. It was just what she wanted – the chance for a new start, the two of them together. They could put the past behind them and look to the future instead.

"I'd like that very much. There's a lot we've still got to learn about one another, but we've got all the time in the world," she replied, slipping her hand into his.

"I tell you what, why don't we take that walk by the creek? My *mamm* doesn't need me to walk her home and I'm not due back at the store. We've got all afternoon," he said.

Naomi felt her heart sing. "I'd like that. I'd like that very much," she replied, and now he offered his arm, and the two of them walked off happily together.

Naomi could only be grateful to Aaron for all he had done for her. He had proved himself the kindest, loyalist, and the most upright man she knew, and the thought of what the future held for them filled her with happiness.

"The cake really was very good. You should make them and sell them," he said.

Naomi laughed. "Don't you be setting up businesses in Faith's Creek, now," she said.

Aaron laughed. "All right, just make them for me," he replied, as she rested her head on his arm.

EPILOGUE

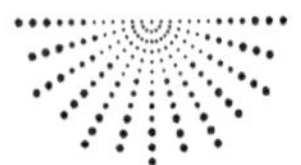

*I*t was six months later, and Naomi and Aaron were married. There had been much happiness and excitement in the community at the announcement, an announcement which had brought with it the news that Don Jacobs had left Faith's Creek and returned to Florida.

There was to be no Tex-Mex restaurant in Faith's Creek, no garage selling RVs, and no visitor center depicting a way of life, that, far from being lost, was thriving. At their wedding ceremony, Bishop Beiler had spoken of marriage as a living tradition, one to be honored and lived in all its fullness with the help of *Gott*, and that was precisely what Naomi and Aaron intended to do.

But one change – amongst others – had come about, and Naomi had taken the lease on the empty wool store. With Aaron's encouragement, she had begun baking cakes for special occasions, of which there were many in Faith's Creek. Aaron had helped her to fit out the store and had built a special display stand for the window, on which she would place her latest creation before its collection. It was becoming something of a spectacle in the marketplace, and many people would stop to admire the latest cake on display.

"You've really found your niche, Naomi. And I get to wave to you from across the marketplace," Aaron had said to her on the day the cake store first opened.

Naomi could not have felt happier, and there was no doubt her reputation was restored. No one now seriously believed she had intended to help Don Jacobs with his malicious schemes, and everyone was happy to see a newly married couple in the community. They lived in a small house just across the road from Aaron's *mamm*. She was a very different person now and looked after herself with ease. She had even started helping Naomi in the cake store, for she had a steady hand, perfect for intricate icing. But there was another happiness to come, one which Naomi and Aaron discovered in the sixth month after they were married. Naomi was pregnant, and she could not wait to reveal the happy news to the quilting circle.

* * *

"You're nearly finished with your quilt, Naomi. You see, I told you it wouldn't take forever. One patch at a time, that's all that's needed," Anna said, as the circle sat together drinking coffee and working on their projects.

Naomi was sitting next to Sarah Beiler, and the others were there, too, with Serena sitting opposite Naomi, working on a blanket with the letters of the alphabet stitched to each square.

"It's lovely, Naomi. You've worked really hard on it," Sarah said.

Naomi smiled. "I'm glad it's nearly finished," she replied.

"And then you can start on something more ambitious. Perhaps a quilt with pictures on it. You could do animals. Cut out the felt shapes and stitch them on," Mary said, and the others nodded.

"I don't know if I'll have time," Naomi replied, for she was uncertain whether the arrival of the *boppli* would mean not only a limit on the number of cakes she could make but also on the time available to attend the quilting circle.

Her aunt looked up at her with a puzzled expression on her face. "Time?" she asked, and Naomi blushed.

"Well... you see, there's something I want to tell you all. Serena knows," she said, for she and Aaron had told his mother the happy news the previous days.

The rest of the circle looked up from their stitching, and Naomi felt embarrassed.

"What is it?" Anna asked.

"Well, you see... there's a reason I've finished the blanket. It's for a *boppli*, the *boppli* Aaron and I are having," she said.

All the other women shrieked in delight.

Naomi's aunt rose to her feet and hurried to put her arms around Naomi and congratulate her.

"Oh, that's wonderful news, Naomi. I'm so happy for you both. Did you know about this, Serena?" she asked, turning to Aaron's *mamm*, who nodded.

"They told me yesterday. I've hardly been able to keep it to myself. It's so exciting, isn't it? I'm so happy for them. A *boppli* brings such joy. I'm going to make a quilt for it, a new one. I've not decided how to decorate it yet, but I'll think of something. I never thought I'd have another *kinner* about the place, but then I never thought Aaron would find the happiness you've brought him, Naomi," she said.

There was much congratulations from everyone, and it was decided by the other women that they would make a special quilt for the *boppli*, and each of them would contribute patches that Naomi's aunt would sew together to complete.

"You've all been so kind," Naomi said when the gathering broke up a short while later.

"Well, it's not like any of us are going to be announcing a *boppli* any time soon," Rebecca said, and the others laughed.

"But we're only too glad to have played matchmaker for you, Naomi. It's brought you such happiness," Susanna said, and the others nodded.

"We should make a habit of it. Who else could we invite to join us? There must be some young women out there we could help," Priscilla said, and Naomi laughed.

"Are you serious?" she said, and her aunt nodded.

"Why not? If we can do it for you, we can do it for anyone," Anna replied, and the others agreed.

Naomi walked home with Serena. She no longer walked with a stick, and she talked animatedly about the plans she had for the future.

"We'll have a nursery set up over here. I'll look after the *boppli* when you and Aaron are working. It's simple enough. I love *kinner*, and it would make me feel useful," she said, as they came to the opposite gates.

Naomi smiled and put her hand on Serena's arm. "Are you sure? I don't want to give up the cake making, but I'm not sure how I'll manage it with a *boppli*, too," she said.

Serena smiled. "Don't you worry. It's about time I did something for Aaron after all these years. And you, Naomi, I'm so pleased he found you. I know it was a bumpy start, but you can't drive a buggy without a few bumps, can you?" she replied.

At that moment, Aaron emerged from their house opposite, carrying a bird box in his hand. He waved to them and came over with a smile on his face.

"I've just finished it. I want to put it up in the garden," he said, and his *mamm* smiled.

"Go on then, I'll just put my shawl inside and come out. You two go," she said, and Aaron offered Naomi his hand.

"Did you tell them?" he asked, as they walked around the side of the house.

"They were thrilled. I'll think we'll have enough quilts for a dozen *bopplis*, let alone one," she replied, laughing.

There was an apple tree in the back garden with long, sturdy boughs. Aaron climbed up into the branches, as Naomi watched from down below. He had a hammer and nails in his back pocket, and he attached the bird box to the tree.

"How's it looking?" he asked.

Naomi peered up through the leaves. "A little to the left, and then your *mamm* can see it when she sits in the garden," she said.

Aaron adjusted the position and hammered in the nails before jumping down.

He came to stand next to Naomi, and the two of them looked up to see the bird box secured above.

"Just right for a new family to move into," he said, putting his arm around Naomi, who smiled.

"I hope they'll be as happy as we are," she said, and he turned to her and kissed her on the forehead.

"I hope so because I couldn't feel happier," he replied.

Naomi felt the same. She could not have been happier than she was at that moment, she had a loving husband, a *boppli* on the way, and the promise of a bright future ahead – all thanks to the quilting circle!

If you enjoyed this book you will love A Love to Heal Her Heart

Faith's Creek, Pennsylvania.

The snow was mesmerizing, falling from the inky dark sky above and blanketing the garden in a pristine covering. The fields around the house appeared as a single expanse of white as far as the eye could see.

Beth Phillips stood at the window, looking out. She had been standing there for an hour or so, just watching the snow fall, thinking of nothing in particular. She liked winter, the warm fires and the cozy nights, the prospect of Christmas to come – though, for her, the season was always twinged with sadness.

It was December, and the first snows had hit hard that year, the ground frozen and the roads around Faith's

Creek icy and treacherous. But Beth had no reason to venture out, the smell of a casserole bubbling on the stove, and the crackle of logs on the fire kept her company as she waited for Isaac's return.

She sighed and pulled the curtain across the window, turning back into the parlor to check all was ready for her husband's arrival. As she did so, she caught sight of herself in the mirror by the porch door. Her long brown hair, always covered by her kapp when outside was hanging down over her shoulders, her wide blue eyes filled with tears.

"You need to cheer up before Isaac comes home," she told herself.

The house was pristine – there was no reason for it not to be. Each morning, after she bid goodbye to Isaac, sending him off to the blacksmith's store with a packet of sandwiches and a flask of coffee, she would make the bed, tidy the parlor, clean down the stove and work her way through a myriad of jobs which designed not only to ensure domestic harmony but also to provide distraction. The house was quiet. It was missing the one thing Beth desired more than anything else in the world: the sound of *kinner*.

The couple had been married for five years, and in those five years, Beth had conceived three times. Each occasion had been a cause for joy and celebration, and each had ended in bitter sorrow and disappointment. There were three *kinner* in Beth's heart, three *kinner* who should have been there now, their voices filling the house, which felt so empty. Every little sound was magnified, not only by the silence of that winter afternoon, but the silence Beth felt at being alone. Each *kinner* had been conceived in love, and each was lost, at rest with *Gott*, and leaving behind it a restless heart in Beth, and a deep sorrow, too.

She longed for a *kinner* to call her own, to hold, and to be a *mamm* to. The names of those three *kinner* were etched on her heart Elijah, Reuben, and Jonah – she thought of each of them every day, and now she glanced across at the mantelpiece, where always she kept three candles burning, one for each of the *kinner* she had lost. A tear ran down her cheek, and she scolded herself for allowing her emotions to overwhelm her. What sort of welcome would that be for Isaac, who was due home at any moment? She did not want him to see she had been crying, and she pulled out her handkerchief and wiped her eyes, just as footsteps on the porch announced his return.

"What a day, it's really come in bad," Isaac said, stomping his boots on the mat, so that the snow flew in white specs on the rug, melting as they hit.

"Oh, well, come inside and warm up. I've just put more wood on the fire. There's a casserole on the stove top, too. You'll soon warm up. How was your day?" Beth asked, coming to kiss him, and taking his hat and coat.

He was a handsome man, four years older than her, with dark hair and dark eyes, and a face which always seemed to smile. Beth loved him with all her heart, and that only magnified the sorrow she felt at not being able to give him the one thing she knew he desired above all else.

"It was all right, but we're going to be hard-pressed to finish the plow repairs for Daniel Graeber before Christmas. He wants the whole thing: stripping back, new parts – we might as well build him a new plow as repair the old one," Isaac replied, pulling off his boots and coming to sit by the fire.

Beth smiled, hoping he would not notice she had been crying. It was the same every day lately. As Christmas approached, she found herself thinking more and more about what they had lost. The house where they lived was close to the schoolhouse, and each morning, Beth would endure the sight of parents taking their little one there, the happy smiles on their faces, the shouts and cries, the laughter – she longed to share in all of that, for she had seen many of her friends become parents and knew the joy their *kinner* brought them.

"I'm sure you'll get it all done. Do you want a drink? Something hot, perhaps? I tried that recipe for mulled apple juice Sarah Beiler gave me. It's delicious," she said.

Isaac nodded. "What did I ever do to deserve you?" he said, smiling at her.

Beth blushed. She did not think herself deserving of Isaac. They had been childhood sweethearts, inseparable, and there had been little doubt in anyone's mind that they would marry. On that happy day, the world had seemed so full of possibility, and they had dreamed of starting a family together. But as the candles on the mantelpiece testified, such dreams had come to nothing. Theirs was a quiet house, and Beth longed for the one thing she could not have – a *kinner* of her own to fill the house with noise.

"I'll just see to the casserole," she said, retreating to the kitchen, as she felt fresh tears welling up in her eyes.

She ladled a cup of the mulled apple juice into a mug, setting it on the side, as she glanced out of the window across the darkening garden which backed onto their neighbor's yard. The Hochstetler's had built a snowman below their porch, with twigs for arms and pieces of coal running up its front as buttons, a carrot was stuck in for a nose, and pebbles made a smiling face and eyes, one of Moses Hochstetler's old hats was pulled down low over its head. She thought of the *kinner* at play, and she reached out and pulled the curtain quickly across the window lest her thoughts overwhelm her once more.

"Are you all right?" Isaac asked, and she jumped, not realizing he had entered the kitchen.

"Oh... I'm all right, it's just getting dark," she said, forcing her face into a smile, and turning to pass him the mug of mulled apple juice.

"And cold, I think we're in for a harsh winter," he said, taking the mug and holding it in both hands.

Beth nodded. She was not sure how much longer she could keep up her charade. Every day it grew harder to put on a brave face and say the right things. Inside, she was hurting, and she had no one but Isaac to confide in. He was so kind and worked tirelessly to provide for her. She felt guilty at the thought of adding to his worries, and she knew he was hurting, too. He did not speak of it, but the pain was clear to see. Sometimes, she would find him staring at the three lit candles, with a look of such sorrow on his face that it broke her heart to see.

"Last year was so mild, it's like the weather's making up for it. It's been years since we've had such snows here," Beth replied, taking the casserole off the stove.

"Maybe we should build a snowman, too," he said, smiling at her, and Beth laughed, remembering happier days when the winter would bring sledding and snow-ball fights.

The past was a far happier place than the present for Beth, and she would often allow her mind to wander, remembering fondly what had been.

"Let's eat," she said, taking two plates from the cupboard and ladling out the casserole.

Grab this amazing box set - 26 Christmas Brides and Seasonal Wishes for FREE with Kindle Unlimited

26
Book
Box Set
CHRISTMAS BRIDES
AND
Seasonal Wishes
unlimited

All my books are FREE on Kindle Unlimited

If you love Amish Romance, the sweet, clean stories of Sarah Miller receive free stories and join me for the latest news on upcoming books here

These are some of my reader favorites:

The Amish Landscape

The Amish Family and Faith Collection

Find all Sarah's books on Amazon and click the yellow follow button

This book is dedicated to the wonderful Amish people and the faithful life that they live.

Go in peace, my friends.

As an independent author, Sarah relies on your support. If you enjoyed this book, please leave a review on Amazon or Goodreads.

ABOUT THE AUTHOR

Sarah Miller was born in Pennsylvania and spent her childhood close to the Amish people. Weekends were spent doing chores; quilting or eventually babysitting in the community. She grew up to love their culture and the simple lifestyle and had many Amish friends. The one thing that you can guarantee when you are near the Amish, Sarah believes is that you will feel close to God.

Many years later she married Martin who is the love of her life and moved to England. There she started to write stories about the Amish. Recently after a lot of persuasion from her best friend she has decided to publish her stories. They draw on inspiration from her relationship with the Amish and with God and she hopes you enjoy reading them as much as she did writing them. Many of the stories are based on true events but names have been changed and even though they are authentic at times artistic license has been used.

Sarah likes her stories simple and to hold a message and they help bring her closer to her faith. She currently lives in Yorkshire, England with her husband Martin and seven very spoiled chickens.

She would love to meet you on Facebook at https://www.facebook.com/SarahMillerBooks

Sarah hopes her stories will both entertain and inspire and she wishes that you go with God.